Me, Jill Robinson

and the Perdou painting

Also by Anne Digby

Me, Jill Robinson
and the Perdou painting

ANNE DIGBY

DRAGON
Granada Publishing

Published by Dragon Hardbacks 1984

Granada Publishing Limited
8 Grafton Street, London W1X 3LA

Copyright © Anne Digby 1963, 1975, 1984

British Library Cataloguing in Publication Data
Digby, Anne
  Me, Jill Robinson and the Perdou painting.
  I. Title
  823'.914[J]   PZ7

ISBN 0-246-12008-8

Printed in Great Britain by
Billing and Sons Ltd, Worcester

Contents

1

❀❀❀

Invited to Tea

'Sarah, you can't go off to college with only a cup of coffee and that ridiculous little roll inside you. You've always had a cooked breakfast in the past. I don't know what's come over you.'

'It's not a ridiculous little roll, Mum,' sighed my big sister, Sarah. 'It's a *croissant*.'

We were all sitting round the breakfast table at 21 Newlands Park. Each member of the family had a plate of bacon and eggs in front of them – except for Sarah. She had just one solitary roll, or croissant, sitting on a small plate beside her cup of coffee.

Now, defiantly, she cut it and spread it with margarine and Gran's home-made plum jam and took her first mouthful.

'Jam at breakfast time!' exclaimed Gran. 'Well I never did!'

'You never did but Sarah *does*, Gran!' I giggled. 'Now she's been to France!'

'Light and flaky and very *nutritious*,' murmured Sarah dreamily, between mouthfuls. 'Honestly, the idea of starting off the day with a heavy, indigestible cooked meal is just too English for words. No wonder the typical Englishman is so dull and bad-tempered in the mornings.'

'Who's bad-tempered?' snapped Dad, looking up

from behind his newspaper. He glared at Sarah. 'What a lot of nonsense you talk, girl.'

As he buried himself back in the newspaper, Sarah glanced round the table with a triumphant smirk. '*See*?' she mouthed at me and Tony, our young brother. Tony and I just held our noses in order not to laugh.

'I can't believe, Sarah love,' said Mum, 'that the sort of breakfast people eat makes any difference to their tempers. And as for starting the day with only coffee and a roll – why, that's not even a breakfast at all. The mornings are still quite cold, you know.'

'Oh, but it is breakfast, Mum,' said Sarah, patiently. 'Millions of people all over France are starting their day *right now* with just the same thing as I am. *Le petit dejeuner*! It's really the civilized thing to do.'

'I've no doubt that millions of people in China are starting off their day eating bamboo shoots with chopsticks,' said Dad drily. 'The Wong-Wing-Bean-feast-Breakfast or something! So why aren't we?'

'Oh, Dad!' said Sarah, looking peeved. 'You're impossible.'

Actually it was Sarah who was impossible. She was now back at Haven college, the new town's tertiary college (where she was doing the Foundation Art course) for the summer term. She'd been becoming progressively more interested in all things French, having fallen under the influence of one of her art teachers who was a Frenchman, but three weeks in Paris over Easter had turned an interest into an obsession.

She was crazy about France. Everything French was wonderful in Sarah's eyes – French films, French architecture, French paintings and now even French breakfasts! There was no doubt that Monsieur Perdou had a lot to answer for. A twitchy, middle-aged Frenchman who didn't get on too well with some of the students – but he and Sarah had apparently developed a marvellous *rapport* (more French). She'd become his favourite pupil and there was no doubt that she, in her turn, was M. Perdou's greatest admirer. We were all pleased that she was so happy at college and apparently blossoming and doing very well. But we *were* getting the wonders of French civilization rammed down our throats a bit!

'Well,' said Sarah, rising to her feet and glancing at her watch, 'I must get going. I promised to be in early this morning.' Her eyes glowed. 'Monsieur Perdou has some points to make about the landscape I finished yesterday. He's promised to go through them with me before lectures.'

'Ooh, la, la!' whistled Tony.

'Vive la France!' I said.

Sarah dived at us and we ducked. 'Stop it, you children!' exclaimed Mum.

Sarah pulled her long rugby sweater down carefully over the hips of her jeans and went off to comb her hair. Then we heard the front door slam.

'Dear Sarah!' said Mum, eyes smiling. Then she glanced at us. 'Come on, you two! Hurry up and eat your breakfasts, or you'll both be late for school.'

'I won't!' said Tony. He was in his last term at Dolphin Avenue primary which was very close to home. 'Jill will, though!'

'Oh, you know what these English breakfasts are like, Mum,' I said, jabbing my bacon with a fork, 'so heavy and indigestible – take hours to eat.'

We all laughed then, Dad included.

Something interesting happened at school that day – school being Haven comprehensive, of course. Polly Pudham – otherwise known as Pudding – invited me home to tea!

Three weeks of the new term had gone by; the netball courts had been switched over to tennis, and the leaves had sprouted on some of the newly planted shrubs and trees in the school grounds which had looked rather bare all winter. It was all beginning to look quite summery.

Pudding had arrived at school on the first day of term as a new girl looking like a fish out of water. Her mother had brought her in a very smart car and shepherded her around the place as if she were five and just starting at primary. Apparently Mr Pudham was rich and was setting up two new factories in Haven. He wanted to be on the spot while they were being built on the industrial estate – it was going to take about two years. So he'd uprooted his wife and Pudding, who was an only child, and brought them to live in Haven – to a house in Millionaires' Row, which is what we called the posh road on the outskirts of the new town, full of grand houses some of which were there when Haven was a village. 'Les-Jen Lodge' was fairly new and was the poshest of the lot – built by a builder called Leslie, apparently, for his third wife whose name was Jennifer. Then they got a divorce and the house was put up for sale (the builder going off to build a new house called 'Les-Mar Lodge' for his fourth wife whose name was Marcia) and it was so expensive that it had stood empty until the rich Pudhams had come along and bought it and moved in, in the Easter holidays.

It was rumoured that they'd had a sauna and an indoor swimming pool put in, and that there was a big revolving circular cocktail bar there that was made of glass and covered with life-like looking lit-up goldfish, so that it seemed as though the goldfish were swimming round in a circle when it spun. The counter above remained stationary, the part you stood your drinks on – which was just as well, I guess.

Poor Pudding had been horribly teased on her first day. She'd been put in 2N, our form, and her mother had informed Miss Rawlings in a carrying voice that:

'There simply isn't a good private school within daily reach and I can't bear the thought of sending Polly away to board – such a problem, don't you think? It's rather an educational desert around here, wouldn't you say?'

And so on.

2N went to town on Pudding after that. Blazers were flung down in her path when she went into the grounds at break –

'It's muddy, your ladyship!'

'Walk this way, Your Highness!'

'Mustn't get your feet soiled in this dreadful place, dahling!'

No wonder the poor girl stuffed her face with crisps and Mars bars from the school vending machines all day. And she couldn't afford to do that because she was rather fat.

No one could have teased her more than Lindy – my best friend, Melinda Hill – and it was really to make up for Lindy that I asked her to give me a knock up at tennis round about the third day. I liked tennis very much, though I wasn't much good at it, but Lindy wasn't keen on tennis at all.

'You're good!' I'd exclaimed to Pudding in some amazement, because she didn't exactly look athletic. 'You must have played a lot. You're much better than me!'

11

I made sure some of the good tennis players found out about it, and before long Pudding was in with the tennis-playing crowd and they were egging her on to enter for the junior cup. She was okay really; she couldn't help her home background.

It was quite a surprise when she came up to me in the dinner hour on this particular day and said:

'Jill, I've been meaning to ask you all week, but it's awkward when you're with Lindy all the time. It's my birthday today – don't tell anyone – and I told Mummy I wanted you to come and have tea with us today, if you'd like to come. I don't suppose you'd like to, would you?'

It was touching really. She looked so nervous. All the same, I didn't fancy it very much.

'Er – '

My momentary dismay must have shown on my face.

'Only – only if you'd like to,' Pudding repeated, looking hurt. 'I'll quite understand if you've other things to do . . .'

'Oh, no!' I said quickly. I felt cross with myself for letting my feelings show. After all, it wasn't Pud's fault if her mother was a snob. 'I'd love to come, it's just you took me by surprise. And I haven't got you a birthday present! I'll have to go home first, of course, so I can tell Mum and change out of school uniform.'

'Of course!' She looked delighted. 'Say five o'clock, then? Daddy will send the car for you.'

'N – no!' I said quickly. I'd joked about Pudding quite a lot at home – I'd never live it down if one of their smart cars rolled up at number 21. 'I'll cycle! I know where your house is. It's called "Les-Jen Lodge", isn't it?'

''Fraid so,' said Pudding. We both laughed. As I say, she was okay really.

Suddenly I realized I was quite looking forward to tea in Millionaires' Row. At least it would be an interesting experience.

What with one thing and another – mainly losing my atlas which I needed for homework and being cross-questioned by Lindy about my surprise invitation – I was late leaving school and didn't get home until half past four.

'Got to rush and get changed!' I exclaimed as I dashed into the house, nearly knocking Gran over. 'Due somewhere for a birthday tea at five o' clock.'

'Bless me!' exclaimed Gran, as I galloped past. 'What with you and Sarah! She's just hugged me and gone rushing up the stairs, looking as if someone's just given her the crown jewels!'

As I washed and scrubbed in the bathroom ready to change into my best cotton dress, I could hear Sarah singing in our bedroom. She was trilling a jolly little French song at the top of her voice, no doubt a favourite of M. Perdou's.

'She *does* sound cheerful!' I thought.

Then as I crossed the landing in my knickers and bra to get dressed, Sarah leapt out of the big room and grabbed my hand.

'Jill, Jill, you must come and see!' Her eyes were wide and starry as she pulled me inside. 'You'll be mesmerised!'

'Honestly, Sar,' I protested. 'See what? I haven't time – I'm late – I've got to find my new stripy dress and – '

'Time? What's time? This is *important*. I insist you

13

come over here and see. Look, by the window. I'm going to show you something so glorious that you'll forget time exists!'

2

❧❧❧

The Perdou Painting

'Can't it wait, Sar?' I asked her. 'I'm going to have tea with someone! She lives the other side of the ring road – and I said I'd cycle!'

I was beginning to wish I'd accepted the offer of the car.

'Please, Jill. You'll be so grateful when I show you what I've got. It's really going to *enrich* you . . .'

Meekly, I allowed Sarah to drag me across to the window sill. A strange looking book lay there. I must admit I was slightly intrigued by now. My sister always spoke in hyperbole when carried away by some enthusiasm or other and there was no doubt that the present enthusiasm was the most powerful I'd seen for ages.

'Look, Jill!' She bounced up and down on her bed holding on tightly to the volume she'd picked up off the window sill. 'Look at this!' Her voice rose to a squeal. 'Oh, isn't it marvellous?'

I peered over her shoulder at the dusty, battered old book she was holding. My spirits sank. How long was this going to take? All the same, I didn't want to hurt Sarah's feelings *too* much.

'Mmm.' I searched for something to say that didn't sound too insincere. 'That looks quite interesting.'

'Quite interesting?' repeated Sarah. She'd opened the book now and was flicking over the pages.

15

Splashes of faded colour kept meeting my eye. The book was full of reproductions of paintings. '*Quite interesting*? It's beautiful – heavenly – unique! You're looking at something unique, Jill! This old French book's completely out of print. It's a hundred years old. And you know something, Jill?' She looked out of the window dreamily and her voice took on a tone of deep reverence. 'This is the *only* book that's ever been published about Perdou.'

'Your art teacher?' I exclaimed, my mouth dropping open.

'No, no, you ignoramus!' she snorted. 'Jean-Paul Perdou, the great nineteenth-century French painter.'

'Perdou?' I said. It was no use pretending. 'Never heard of him.'

'You've never heard of *Perdou*?' asked Sarah, scornfully. But there was something about the way she wouldn't meet my eye that suggested that she'd only heard about him herself quite recently. 'Perdou was the greatest of all the French Impressionist painters. He was born about a hundred and fifty years ago. Let me see . . .'

She closed her eyes, concentrated, then opened them and started ticking things off on her fingers.

'Yes, he was born in 1838. Just after Manet and Degas, just before Monet and Renoir.'

'I've heard of *them*!' I said in relief, doing my best to look intelligent and interested. 'They were painters, too, weren't they? That ballet print in Mum and Dad's room, isn't that by Degas?'

'They were painters all right, of a sort,' said Sarah scornfully. 'Their reputation has become quite inflated over the years. But the truth is – ' she paused importantly ' – that beside Perdou they pale into insignificance. His work outstrips theirs in every way.'

16

More ticking off on fingers. 'Manet had feeling for the actuality of colour, but Perdou had more. Renoir had a tremendous robust animalism, but Perdou had more. Degas had – '

'Amazing, Sar!' I could feel a big yawn coming and had to stifle it. 'He must have been a genius.'

'He was,' Sarah replied shortly. 'Look at some of these pictures.'

She flicked through the book, showing me the reproductions of Perdou's paintings. One or two of them were quite pleasant, especially one of an old French chateau, all misty and surrounded by trees, but most of them looked a mess to me.

'If he's so marvellous,' I asked innocently, 'why's there only ever been this one book published about him?'

'Because,' Sarah said witheringly, 'genius is not always recognized at once. It takes time . . .'

'But if he was born a hundred and fifty years ago, surely he's had enough time to be discovered by now?'

'Don't worry, he will be,' Sarah said crossly. Then a soppy look came into her eyes. 'Monsieur Perdou – this is his book, you know, he's lent it to me as a special favour – says it could be any time in the next few years. The fact is, Perdou was born a hundred and fifty years ahead of his time. And want to know something else, Jill? Jean-Paul Perdou was Monsieur Perdou's *great-grandfather*! Isn't that amazing?'

I suppressed a smile. I'd guessed at once who'd lent Sarah the book and for the last five minutes I'd been trying to work out what kind of a relation the un-known painter was to her revered art teacher. But I said, tactfully, 'Monsieur Perdou's great-grandfather? That really is amazing, isn't it!'

'I've got to give this back to Monsieur Perdou in the

morning, that's why I wanted you to look at it now, Jill. It's the only chance you'll get. He never ever lends this book around as a rule. It's *very* precious to him. It's the only record he has of his great-grandpa's paintings. Isn't it tragic?

'When Perdou died, all his work was sold to pay off his debts; and even the family home had to be sold as well, a beautiful old French chateau! Monsieur Perdou's searched museums and art galleries to track down some of the paintings, but – '

'Must find my dress, Sar!' I exclaimed.

As I rummaged in the wardrobe, found the dress and pulled it on, Sarah was still absorbed in the book and babbling away.

'There's a picture of the chateau in here. It had been the family home for five hundred years! It was in the Loire valley. Monsieur Perdou went to find it once but apparently it had been destroyed by fire in 1900.'

'Maybe that's what's happened to all the paintings, too – ' I began, then put my hand to my mouth as I realized what I'd said. 'I mean, maybe they were in some art gallery and it got bombed in the second world war? Or something. Anyway – thanks for showing me the book, Sar. It's really . . . . Got to rush now, going to be late!'

As I pedalled round town towards Millionaires' Row and the Pudhams' house, I laughed to myself quite a lot. Jean-Paul Perdou was M. Perdou's great-grandfather! That explained Sarah's sudden craze for a painter that no one else had ever heard of!

The Pudhams' magnificent house was set in about an acre of gardens, like all the houses in this particular road. Some of them were solid, dignified-looking places that had been there since Edwardian times.

Pudding's snobbish mum, furious at being dragged away from London, had insisted on something new, and if possible the most expensive house in Haven, as compensation for having to come and live somewhere so far from Harrods while Mr Pudham was supervising the building of his new factories in Haven.

I found Mrs Pudham a real pain, but poor Pudding couldn't help having a mother like that. I wondered what her father was going to be like!

As I cycled up the drive towards Les-Jen Lodge the fragrant scent of roses filled the evening air. A professional landscape gardener had laid out the whole thing two years previously, Pudding had explained to me, specially for Les's new wife Jen. The house was by far the newest in the road, and architect-designed. White and cubic with lots and lots of glass – the architect must have been used to designing boxes!

A girl (a foreign au pair) opened the front door. Pudding was just behind her.

Like me, she'd changed out of her school uniform. She was now wearing a smart blue shirt-dress that suited her height and made her look a lot slimmer. There was no trace now of that plump, sullen look about the face that had helped to make her such a joke when she'd arrived at school three weeks before. But of course she'd settled in and was feeling happier now, and seemed to have stopped completely that business of eating all the time to cheer herself up. I'd told her she ought to count to fifty before going near any of the vending machines and she'd taken my advice seriously. It seemed to have worked.

'Sorry I'm late, Pud,' I exclaimed.

'That's all right, Jill. I was only worried you might

have changed your mind. About coming. Tea's all ready, I'll take you through.'

My feet sank into heavy pile carpet as she took me down a long, wide reception hall, then up some marble steps and through to a huge sunlit drawing room. One wall was entirely of glass, with a terrace outside, and beyond – a view of the grounds, then open country-side. This side of the house faced away from the town. The afternoon sun was filtering through cloud, casting a hazy light over the distant fields.

Tea was set out on a low table. There was a silver teapot and dainty bone china cups, and lots of little cakes and sandwiches. In the middle, a mouth-water-ing chocolate gateau. Both Pudding's parents were in the room. Her mother was wearing a lilac jump-suit, big earrings and lots of make-up. Her father looked rather scruffy. His shirt had come open in the middle and his stomach was bulging through. He was red-faced and was smoking a cigar.

'How d'you do, lass,' he said, rising to his feet and stubbing out the cigar. 'I've heard a lot about you from our Polly.'

I was rather surprised at his broad accent – Mrs Pudham spoke in such a refined la-di-da way. Ob-viously her husband had made all his money himself by being hard-headed and clever in business. I noticed he had shrewd, rather cold eyes.

'You're late, Jill,' Mrs Pudham said, in a clipped voice, as she started to pour out tea. 'We were getting quite concerned.'

'Sorry,' I said, awkwardly. 'The fact is I got caught by my sister. She's at the tertiary college, doing the Foundation Art course. She's – well – crazy about these paintings. She insisted on showing me some of them in a book.'

20

'Alfred is interested in the arts, aren't you dear?' said Mrs Pudham, still pouring. She glanced at her husband. 'He collects things. He bought a painting in London this morning! It's an original, of course. He only buys originals. We've put it in the back lobby. Unfortunately, it's *rather* hideous. But the frame's good. Quite an antique.'

'Aye. But it's not what a painting looks like that matters. They all look the same to me.' Mr Pudham's voice was jolly as his wife passed him a cup of tea, a smug smile spreading across his face. 'It's the brass in 'em. Put a bit o' milk in my tea, Queenie.'

'Oh, Dad, I wish you wouldn't call Mummy that!' protested Pudding.

'Brass?' I asked, puzzled. I was wondering how a painting could have brass in it. Then Pudding caught my eye, looking embarrassed.

'Daddy means money,' she said. 'You know. How much they're worth.'

'Aye. Now take this painting I bought today. I picked it up from a dealer in London for fifty quid. Only fifty! But I'd been tipped off, you see.' He leant forward and tapped on the table triumphantly. 'I've got a good friend in the art world who always tells me when a painter's on the up and up. Know what I mean? And I'll tell you something else. Two or three years from now I'll be able to sell this picture I bought today for mebbe twenty times what I paid for it. Like to know how much I made – '

'Oh, Daddy! Jill doesn't want to hear all this!' said Pudding.

'So your sister's an artist?' Mrs Pudham's well-bred voice chipped in. It seemed that she was anxious to change the subject, too. 'How very interesting. Do you come from an artistic family, Jill?' she asked. 'I

21

expect you'd like to see our new painting after tea. Of course, it's nothing special.'

I seemed to be plagued with Art from all directions!

'I'm afraid I wouldn't be able to tell, even if it was,' I said.

'I expect Jill'd rather come up to my room,' Pud said hurriedly, reading the expression on my face. 'I want to play my new cassette!'

'Be quiet, Poll,' snapped Mr Pudham. 'If the lass's sister's an artist then she'll be wanting to see my new painting. Am I right or wrong, Jill?'

'I – er – ' Quickly I recovered my manners. 'I'd love to see the painting.'

'Right!' He nodded. 'Then you shall.' He made it seem as though he were the one doing *me* a favour!

Tea was delicious, especially that cake. Words can't describe it!

And after tea, they led me through the house to the back lobby place. Mr Pudham pointed to the painting, which hung on a wall opposite a small window. Pudding fidgeted, looking bored. Her mother disappeared.

The painting was in oils and the subdued light brought out the faded mistiness of its blues and greys rather eerily. It had a striking, long-ago quality, but there was also something familiar about it – I felt as though I knew the place depicted.

'There she is! Not much to look at, I dare say. But worth a bit o' brass later on. That's if my little flutter comes off. It's signed, you know.'

He walked over and stabbed near the bottom of the canvas with his forefinger.

'There's the signature. The name of the picture's written on the back of the frame, too. The artist wrote it in the same hand.'

He took it off the wall and turned it over. There, written on the back of the frame were the words: *Le Chateau Perdou – 1875*.

As Pudding's father returned the oil painting to the wall a shiver of recognition went through me. I peered closely at the signature in the bottom right hand corner: J-P Perdou.

'How amazing,' I said.

3

❀ ❀ ❀

A Date at
'Les-Jen Lodge'

'Amazing?' asked Pudding, looking bewildered.
'Why?'

'It's by Jean-Paul Perdou – signed and everything!'
I said, but just to myself. 'No doubt about it. The
chateau in the Loire valley – the family home that
Sarah was talking about! It was in the book, and this is
it. The original!'

'Famous painting, you think?' asked Mr Pudham.
'Good buy, eh? You know the painting, then?' He
rubbed his hands. 'I can spot 'em, Poll, can't I?'

'Not famous especially, Mr Pudham,' I said. 'Just,
well, just an amazing coincidence!'

Mr Pudham stared at me. 'How d'ya mean, lass?'

Mrs Pudham had appeared in the lobby. She looked
approving once more.

'I'm most impressed, Jill,' she said. 'I can see you
come from a very *cultured* family indeed. To know
about such an obscure work of art! Of course, I think
the painting's rather plain, but I do like to have
culture in the house.'

'Who said anything about it being obscure?' snapped her husband – and Pudding just stood there
writhing with embarrassment.

Her mother spoke of 'culture' as though it were

some sort of consumer durable like a washing machine or a video recorder!

'Oh, Mummy.' Pud glared at her mother, who was just gliding out of the room again. Then she gave me a little nudge with her elbow. 'Come off it, Jill, you're not all that interested in art.' She was a bit puzzled. 'How d'you know about the painting? What d'you mean about it being an amazing coincidence and being in a book or something?'

I giggled. I'd been feeling so knowledgeable and important – now Pudding had spoiled it!

'As a matter of fact I don't know much about art at all,' I admitted. 'But my sister Sarah does – well, a bit – and she showed me this book of reproductions, you see. Just before I left the house! That's why I was late, remember? All the pictures in the book were by a certain painter. Guess who?'

'Perdou!' exclaimed Pudding.

'Right!' I nodded. 'He was born in eighteen thirty something. He's the least well-known of the French Impressionists,' I added, putting it politely – and airing my new-found knowledge. 'Sarah got the book from her art teacher, he's French, and his name's Perdou as well! Apparently the artist was his great-grandfather. It's a terribly old book and the only one that's ever been published about Perdou.' I bent my head close to Pudding's ear and whispered: 'I didn't like most of the paintings in the book, but I remembered this one all right because it sort of had atmosphere. It's even nicer, seeing the real thing.'

'*Le Chateau Perdou* – you saw it in this book?' Pud exclaimed. She looked at the painting on the wall with fresh interest, and whistled. 'You're right, Jill. What a coincidence! It *is* an amazing coincidence, that

Daddy's just bought the original.' She turned to her father. 'Isn't it, Daddy?'

But her father was frowning at the painting, and looking business-like. He was mainly interested in the financial aspect.

'Only one book been published about him?' he said. 'Hope he's some good, then!'

'I haven't told you the rest of the coincidence yet,' I continued, my excitement mounting. 'Why Sarah and her art teacher are so interested in Perdou. You see, not only is Monsieur Perdou the great-grandson of Jean-Paul Perdou, but he's been searching for years just to set eyes on an original. And this one's the best of the lot! It was the family home – '

'How very interesting, Jill,' interrupted Mrs Pudham, who had just returned, snobbery bursting out all over her. 'The painter's great-grandson – living *here*! In this cultural desert! Teaching at the art college.'

'The tertiary college!' I corrected her, then rushed on: 'The chateau was destroyed! Oh, can't you imagine how thrilled Monsieur Perdou would be if he knew this painting was here – in Haven, in the very town where he's living? You see,' I explained, 'all the paintings were sold when the artist died, to pay off his debts or something. Poor Monsieur Perdou hasn't been able to track down a single one yet! The only proper record he's got of his great-grandfather's work is this book he's lent my sister.'

I think most of what I was saying had escaped Pudding's mother. But she looked pleased.

'I know what we'll do!' she said. 'We'll invite him to the house, to see the painting. Your sister, too. How intriguing! I'd no idea there was such a cultured man living in Haven. Jill, poppet, you must fix it up!'

26

Poppet! I appeared to have gone up in her estimation by leaps and bounds.

'Thanks, Mrs Pudham!' I said. 'I'd love to!'

I meant what I said. Without being much interested in Perdou's paintings myself, I'd do anything for my sister Sarah, and she'd usually do anything for me. I was longing to see her face when I broke the news to her that one of M. Perdou's ancestor's paintings was here in Haven! How she'd revel in the excitement of having something so impressive to tell *him*!

'Aye, you arrange it, lass,' said Mr Pudham, thoughtfully. 'I'd like to meet this man. He'll be able to tell me the exact market value of Perdou's paintings. He'll tell me whether I've got a good buy or not.'

'Oh, *Daddy*!' sighed Pudding. Then she linked arms with me. 'Come on, Jill! Let's go upstairs – there's loads of things to do.'

Pudding had a beautiful room upstairs. I was really envious. We had a good time, playing some computer games and messing about with her electronic organ and then re-running a TV programme I'd wanted to see the previous weekend but had missed because of Dad and his cricket. I didn't mind in the least forgetting about art and paintings for a couple of hours!

All the same, I thought how cosy 21 Newlands Park looked when I cycled back home – even if it did suddenly seem rather small, after Les-Jen Lodge.

Sarah had gone to bed early for once and she was fast asleep when I went upstairs, so I wasn't able to break the news to her until breakfast time next morning.

When I told her, she almost choked over her croissant.

'Jill!' she spluttered. 'You don't *mean* it? An original Perdou, here in Haven? The one of the old chateau? Oh, *Jill*! Are you *sure*? It's not a forgery, is it?' Her voice rose to a pitch of excitement. 'Just wait till I tell him! Oh, Jill – what does it look like? Do you like it? Tell me about the texture! Tell me anything . . .!'

'It's nice, Sar,' I said quite truthfully, for I did think the painting was pretty. 'It's like in the book, only the colours are much more subtle when you see them in the original. Sort of faded and misty. Lovely soft blues and greys.'

'Of course, of course,' Sarah nodded. She reached down to her bag and then gingerly took out a cardboard box. The book was inside, wrapped in tissue paper, ready to take back to M. Perdou. She unwrapped it, then carefully thumbed through until she found the reproduction of *Le Chateau Perdou*. 'Yes, here it is. But of course no reproduction can do justice to an original oil painting. Not really. And you've actually *seen* it? Oh, Jill, you lucky thing!'

Bursting with importance, I broke the news – that Mr and Mrs Pudham had said Sarah and M. Perdou could come to the house and look at the painting, and that I was to fix it all up.

'Jill!' Sarah cried. Leaping up from the table she rushed round and hugged me. 'You angel! Wonderful!'

'Sarah! Do sit down and finish your coffee!' exclaimed Mum, coming through with Dad's cooked breakfast. 'Leaping around like a jack-in-the-box – what's the matter with you?'

'It's all this French food,' said Gran. 'You'll get

indigestion, Sarah. Those little croissants are very indigestible on an empty stomach.'

'Oh, Gran!' I laughed. 'You've got it all wrong!'

'The sooner you've finished your art course the better, if you ask me,' mumbled Dad from behind his newspaper. He'd never been very enthusiastic about Sarah going to Haven college. 'You seem to have gone quite silly this term. All Frenchified, and your clothes get more ridiculous all the time. I'm not sure this Monsieur Perdou's a good influence.'

'Sarah's in love!' Tony sniggered. 'Sarah's smitten! Sarah's got a crush!'

'*You'll* be smitten in a moment!' retorted Sarah, who at any other time would certainly have clipped Tony's ear for that. But today she just giggled.

My news had put her in a very good mood.

I smiled as I wheeled my bike out and watched her going up the road a few minutes later. She was wearing bright scarlet jeans, topped by a man's suit jacket and a sort of pork-pie hat atop her fair hair. She skipped all the way up the road, her bag swinging jauntily on her arm.

Of course, I told Lindy the whole amazing story at school that day. She thought it was really exciting.

It was arranged that the three of us should go to Pudding's house on Saturday afternoon – me, Sarah and M. Perdou.

We'd arranged to meet the art teacher at Cobbers, the coffee bar in the town centre, first. Sarah and I went down there on our bikes.

'I must say I'm dying to meet him, Sar,' I said as we

cycled along. 'After all, I *have* heard quite a lot about him!'

'You'll like him, Jill!' she said confidently. 'He's a wonderful person. And you've no idea how emotional he is about seeing this painting. He practically *trembled* when I told him about it!'

'Did you say he's coming by bike, too?' I asked. 'Somehow I'd imagined him having a car. A smart French sports car!'

'Oh, no, Jill, he's not like that at all!' Sarah laughed. 'He bikes everywhere. He hasn't got a car. In fact, he always seems poverty-stricken, as though he were still a student or something, even though he's quite old.'

'Really?'

'Yes, really.' Sarah was being serious now. 'It's a shame – he just hasn't got much money. He lives in a bed-sitter, I gather, on the other side of town. I think he's got parents in France who are very elderly and have health problems – so his salary helps to support them. And as if that isn't bad enough, he's paying off some family debt to do with his father's business going bust.'

We reached the civic centre and propped our bikes up outside Cobbers. There was a very old-fashioned looking bike propped up there already – a gent's black Raleigh, the sit-up-and-beg kind, usually only exported to Ireland and Nigeria these days. I rather like them, actually.

Sarah peered eagerly through the windows of the coffee bar.

'He's inside!' she exclaimed happily. 'Come on, Jill!'

As we pushed through the swing doors, out of the sunshine and the fresh air and into the subdued lighting and smoky atmosphere of Cobbers, it took me a few moments to see about me. The sun had dazzled me.

From the juke box came the heavy beat of rock music. Cobbers was full of Haven's young unemployed, drinking tea and coffee and whiling away Saturday afternoon. Keeping out of the sun and hoping that Saturday night would be good.

Then, from behind a table in an alcove, a figure rose and came forward to greet us. He looked strangely out of place – a middle-aged man, quite a lot older than Dad, even. But, all the same, he was very handsome, even though he had a rather drawn, twitchy look about him. His face was thin and sensitive; well-lined, but the lines were quite attractive. He had thick, wavy hair. It was grey. His eyebrows were bushy and very black. He was wearing dark purple corduroy trousers, a green denim shirt that hung loose over the top of his trousers, and a black leather tie.

Heads turned as he came towards us, for he certainly did have a very striking appearance. Sarah was glowing radiantly, like a sun-worshipper suddenly in the presence of the sun.

'Jill, this is Monsieur Perdou,' she whispered. Then she pushed me forward slightly. 'My young sister, Jill.'

'How do you do, Jill.' His English was flawless. To my surprise he took hold of my hand and pressed it to his lips. 'I see you are as beautiful as your sister. Some time I must paint you.'

'H-how do you do,' I stammered. I felt embarrassed and awkward. I was sure my face had gone red. Some of the boys in Cobbers whistled. 'Sar's talked about you a lot,' I managed to say.

'Oh, Jill.' Now it was Sarah's turn to look embarrassed. 'Shut up.' Then she gazed at M. Perdou. 'Isn't it wonderful about the painting? I can hardly believe we're actually going to see it this afternoon!'

'The painting!' The Frenchman sighed ecstatically. 'Ah, yes, the painting. Come – ' He gazed round Cobbers rather distastefully. 'Let us leave this little *bistro*. I do not find it completely *sympathique*. But then – ' He gave a rich, low laugh. 'I am an old man, am I not?'

Jauntily he paid for his coffee and led us outside, one on each arm. We paused before mounting our bikes.

'Jill!'

He stared at me, a tremendously intense expression in his dark eyes. Now we were out in the sunlight I could see his face more clearly, and I could see that a very emotional, highly-strung personality lay behind that face.

'Yes, Monsieur Perdou?' I prompted shyly.

'I cannot find the words to thank you,' he said, 'for putting this opportunity in my path. I will be frank, I sometimes feared that one day I would die – ' he paused and his words quivered in the air, full of emotion ' – yes, die – without having seen one of my great-grandfather's paintings. When your sister told me the news, that one of your young school friends has this painting in her house . . .' he pressed a hand against his chest . . . 'My heart, it almost stops.'

'And it's one of Perdou's best works, isn't it?' said Sarah in a hushed voice, catching the mood of reverence. 'The portrait of your old ancestral home in the Loire valley, before it was destroyed by fire!'

'Yes. We were a great family once,' he whispered, with sadness. He fell silent for a moment. Then: 'Come. Let us go,' he said.

32

As we cycled off round the back of the civic centre and on to the inner ring road, I must admit I felt pretty pleased with myself, like a fairy godmother or something. Not that I'd actually done anything. It had just been an amazing coincidence. But even so! To bring someone so much happiness . . .

It had been simple enough to arrange this meeting. But what joy it would bring, by the look of things!

'Mrs Pudham's longing to meet both of you,' I said, by way of conversation, as we cycled along Millionaires' Row towards the Pudhams' house a few minutes later. 'Especially you, Monsieur Perdou,' I added shyly. 'She thinks Haven's rather devoid of culture and she's still reeling at the thought that a descendant of a genuine French Impressionist painter's living in the town. Apparently she's been talking about it all week.'

'If they're patrons of the arts, there might be so many ways they could help you!' said Sarah wistfully.

But the Frenchman was hardly listening to our words. We'd turned in through the brilliant gold-painted wrought-iron gates of Les-Jen Lodge and were cycling up the drive to the front entrance of the house.

He was staring at the house, which was garishly modern and full of sharp angles. He was staring, too, at the big flash car that stood outside. Just for a moment I saw it all through his eyes.

'Your friends, they have not very much – let us say – taste?'

'Well, perhaps more money than taste,' I replied with a grin.

But as we dismounted and propped up our cycles outside the house, there was no answering smile from

M. Perdou. He was staring darkly at the house, shaking his head.

'My beloved painting,' I heard him say under his breath. 'I hope it is in the right hands. I hope it is deeply appreciated.'

I'd been so looking forward to our date at 'Les-Jen Lodge', but from that moment on I had a feeling of foreboding.

4

❀ ❀ ❀

An Embarrassing Scene

'The chateau,' he whispered hoarsely, quite overcome with emotion.

We were in the Pudhams' back lobby. But there was such an air of hushed reverence created by Sarah and M. Perdou that I felt as though I were in church!

There was no doubt that the painting had atmosphere, and as I looked at it, just for a few moments, the atmosphere began to grip me. The mistiness of that long-ago chateau filled me with a kind of sadness, the sadness of knowing that it had been burnt to the ground and that even if I went to France and searched the whole length of the great river valley I'd never be able to see it, touch it, enter or explore it. The thought of that made me ache with a kind of longing – it was ridiculous, really. After all, it hadn't been the Robinsons' family seat or anything, had it? Yet I had a glimmer of how M. Perdou must be feeling at this moment, just a glimmer.

It quickly passed.

The solemn atmosphere engendered by Sarah and M. Perdou began to get a bit heavy as they stood there, just gazing at the picture without moving. Pudding and I stepped back, politely. I liked the painting, but could never be moved by it the way that they could. As for Mr and Mrs Pudham, they were shifting from one foot to another, getting very bored and fidgety.

'The home of my ancestors,' whispered M. Perdou. He moved at last, tip-toeing forward and gently touching the canvas with his long, delicate fingers. 'The texture, the colours, the composition, everything . . . quite perfect. *Formidable!*'

'I know nowt about art,' broke in Mr Pudham. It was rather crude of him, to say the least, I thought. 'One splosh of colour is just like the next, to me. What I'd like you to tell me is this: what's the market value? I want to know if I've got a bargain or not.'

Slowly, M. Perdou turned round and looked at Mr Pudham. It was as though he had been rudely awakened from a very beautiful dream. He obviously couldn't believe his ears.

'I did not quite catch – ?'

Mr Pudham repeated his question.

'Market value?' M. Perdou almost spat the words out. 'It is priceless!'

'Priceless?' said Mr Pudham eagerly. 'But how many pounds – just tell me roughly, man . . .'

'I have absolutely no idea,' snapped M. Perdou then. He said that roughly all right! But everyone noticed the look of withering distaste he gave Pudding's father – everyone except for Mr Pudham himself, that is.

M. Perdou turned back to the painting, touching it once more, with protective tenderness. 'A true work of art cannot be valued in terms of money. And this is a true work of art.'

'Aye, that's what I like to hear,' beamed Mr Pudham in his thick-skinned way. 'Sounds as though I've done myself a bit o' good.'

'Er – Mummy – ' Pudding tugged at her mother's sleeve, looking very embarrassed. 'Shall we take them in for tea now?'

'A good idea, darling!' exclaimed Mrs Pudham, clearly bored stiff by all this. She'd been expecting M. Perdou to look distinguished, and he looked scruffy. 'It's all set out in the other room.'

We all trooped out of the big lobby then – all except M. Perdou. He remained behind, still gazing raptly at the painting. There was something about him that made it quite clear he did not want to be disturbed for the time being.

In the drawing room we sat and drank tea, and I gazed at the panoramic view of the countryside through the huge glass wall that led on to the terrace. The atmosphere became much jollier as we chatted. Sarah was very good, keeping up a steady stream of conversation with Mrs Pudham about clothes and fashion. Mr Pudham asked me how I was getting on at school. He seemed in a very good mood now, too.

It was a full ten minutes before M. Perdou entered the room. He'd obviously been gazing at the painting all that time. As he came in, the conversation somehow petered out and then came to a full stop.

The Frenchman's eyes were dark and troubled. There was an intense, nervous look about him. His grey hair was ruffled. He walked over and sat on the arm of Mr Pudham's chair.

'Mr Pudham,' he said jerkily. 'How much did you pay for the painting? I have a reason for asking.'

'Fifty pounds,' the north-country man replied flatly.

'Then – ' M. Perdou was trembling with excitement. He pulled a cheque book out of his pocket. 'See . . . I am not a rich man, but I have a little money put by. I must have the painting. I will give you the fifty pounds. It is all I have,' he added simply.

He sounded so pathetic, it was embarrassing. I stared at the floor. I was remembering what Sarah had told me – that he lived in a miserable little bed-sitter and that most of his salary from college went to support his old parents in France.

But if there were any tension in the air, it was quite lost on Mr Pudham. He snorted.

'Fifty pounds – same that I paid for it? You must be joking! Nothing doing.' He threw back his head and laughed; though his eyes didn't laugh – they were as hard and cold as marbles. 'I've bought that thing as an investment. That's what I get my little bit of fun from, y'see. Why, you told me yourself it was priceless! Ha! Ho!' He laughed again, loudly, at his own joke. 'We'll have to see about that. But if your relative comes into fashion, as I've been told he will, I'll make a fat profit, won't I?'

End of conversation – almost.

'I could raise a hundred pounds,' said M. Perdou, desperately.

'Sorry, sir.' The voice was tough now. 'I'm hanging on.'

Pudding coughed. Sarah tried to start up a fresh conversation, but failed miserably. Even Mrs Pudham seemed to sense the – well – slight awkwardness!

'Tea, Monsieur Perdou?' she asked, with a bright, sweet smile.

The Frenchman was staring into space. It took several seconds for Mrs Pudham's words to impinge. Then he turned slowly on his heel. He looked troubled and upset.

'*Non, merci*. No – thank you very much,' he said, in a voice scarcely louder than a whisper. 'I do not think I wish to stay in this place to tea.'

Then with a few sudden strides he'd crossed the room and gone out of the door. Before any of us had recovered from our surprise we heard the distant reverberation of the front door which he'd slammed loudly behind him, presumably.

Sarah jumped up, catching in her breath.

'Monsieur Perdou!' she cried hoarsely, into the empty air.

I just sat there, my legs feeling leaden, and couldn't meet Pudding's eye. What an embarrassing scene it had all turned into. How I wished I'd never set eyes on that wretched painting now! I really regretted ever having mentioned its existence!

But in the weeks to come I was going to regret it even more, the way things turned out.

5

✿✿✿

Sarah's Sweet Idea

'Come back!' Sarah cried shrilly.

She rushed across the big room and out of the door, and I raced after her, down the marble steps. We ran the whole length of the spacious, thickly-carpeted hall to the front door and Sarah dragged it open.

'Monsieur Perdou!' she shouted, cupping her hands to her mouth. 'Please come back . . .'

Her voice trailed off into silence.

We could both see the back view of the distant figure pedalling away down the drive on the erect black bicycle. His shoulders were hunched slightly over the handlebars, the breeze lifting his thick grey hair. He didn't once glance back towards the house, just pumped at the pedals furiously. Within moments he'd turned out of the drive, into the road, and was lost from view behind the high beech hedge that screened Les-Jen Lodge from the road.

'It's no use,' I said. 'He's gone.'

'Yes, he's gone,' repeated Sarah, in a daze.

Without speaking, we returned indoors and made our way back to the drawing room where we were supposed to be sitting quietly and having our polite cup of tea with the Pudhams. They were waiting there, looking very discomfited.

'Strange fellow,' said Mr Pudham, just a little too

heartily. 'Dashing off like that. Not stopping to have tea or owt. Seemed right upset.'

'Of course he was, darling,' said Mrs Pudham. Her over-refined voice contrasted oddly with her husband's broad accents. 'Such an artistic man. He seemed to have fallen in love with our painting. And he was so astonished when you refused to sell it to him.'

'Aye.' A steely edge crept into Mr Pudham's voice now. He was on the defensive. 'But why should he be astonished? Just because the painting was the work of his great-grandfather didn't give him the right to buy it from me.' His lips set in a stubborn line. 'That was a right bargain, that painting. And I'm sticking to it. If I sell it in a few years' time, when this fellow Perdou comes into fashion, I'll make a big profit.' He looked at his wife sharply. 'You know that's the only reason I buy art.'

'Of course, dear, of course.' Mrs Pudham flashed her husband a bright smile, as though eager to show she was on his side.

Pudding just stared at the carpet and wouldn't meet my eye.

Sarah had been silent, but now she recovered her composure.

'I – I'm sorry he made a scene,' she said, though she was looking more tight-lipped than sorry, really. 'He's a very, very highly-strung person. You see, as I think I told you, all his great-grandfather's paintings were sold after he died, to pay off his debts or something. When the chateau was sold, I suppose. Monsieur Perdou's been trying to trace them ever since. It's an obsession – he's spent half his life looking for them. Just to see them! Of course, he'd like to own some too,

I expect, especially this one you've got here. But he knows he hasn't any money. He just wants to be able to look at them, know where they are, know they're in good hands. Well, almost as though they were his babies! Then the shock of finding one at last – I'm sure he didn't mean to be rude like that,' Sarah ended, lamely. She paused. Then: 'I'm sure he'll write a note and apologize, when he realizes.'

Mr Pudham scowled but gradually the atmosphere un-froze, thanks to Sarah's tact. We drank tea and made general conversation, and pretended that nothing had happened.

Before it was time for us to leave, Pudding and I went for a stroll on the big terrace outside. It was warm and sunny.

'I'm sorry about everything, Jill,' she said, with some awkwardness. 'Wasn't it awful? Of course, anyone else would have sold Monsieur Perdou the painting, or even given it to him, seeing how much it means to him. But Daddy's hard as nails when it comes to money. That's how he's done so well,' she confided. 'He started off in life with nothing, and has had to fight all the way. You wouldn't believe it,' she ended loyally, 'but he can be really kind and nice in other ways. At least, I think so!'

'It's not your fault, Pudding!' I said quickly. 'If it's anyone's, it's mine.' I spoke feelingly. 'I thought it was such a great idea, arranging for Monsieur Perdou to come and have a look at the painting. But all it's done is make him miserable. I just wish I'd never mentioned it in the first place, that's all!'

But when we got back into the house, the others suddenly seemed in a cheery mood. We tracked them down in the big back lobby. It was full of sun. Sarah was standing in front of the painting, and speaking animatedly to Pud's parents. Her eyes were shining. She never stayed down-hearted for long!

'Can I really do that? Really? Oh, thank you!'

'Of course, dear girl,' said Mrs Pudham, obviously anxious to redeem the credentials of the inmates of Les-Jen Lodge. 'We are only too pleased to help young persons interested in the *arts*, in any way we can.'

She rolled the word 'arts' round her tongue with obvious delight.

'Oh, thanks!' Sarah seemed really excited. 'I'll come tomorrow evening, then! It shouldn't take me more than a few evenings. It'll be wonderful practice for me, won't it?'

Then it was time to go. As we cycled home together, Sarah explained what she was up to.

'I'm going to make a life-size copy of the painting, in oils,' she said excitedly – we were pedalling quite fast and she was a little breathless. 'Oh, Jill – it'll be a good exercise for me, won't it? But that isn't really why I want to do it! It's more than that. I'm going to do it specially to cheer up Monsieur Perdou.'

'Cheer him up?'

'Yes.' She was staring at the road ahead, a downhill bit now, smiling dreamily. 'I know he'll be proud when he realizes the painting moved me so much that I just *had* to make a copy of it! Did you know, Jill, that's the highest compliment you can pay an artist?'

I hadn't known that.

'What's more,' she lowered her voice, confidingly, 'I'm hoping that my doing this will sort of make up to him. For his disappointment, I mean. And he might even like to keep my copy. Do you think he will? Do you think, if I can get it really close to the original, he will?'

'Oh Sar, how do I know?' I said.

Dear Sarah! It was certainly a sweet idea; my big sister's quite a sweet person. But – a copy! Somehow I doubted very much whether a *copy* would ever make up for M. Perdou's disappointment. It would just rub salt in the wound, wouldn't it – remind him of an afternoon that would be much better forgotten.

But I could hardly say that to her, could I? And in any case, when Sarah gets an idea in her head common sense is the last thing that will shift it.

6

❀ ❀ ❀

Term Passes

My pessimism turned out to be well-founded.

Sarah visited the Pudhams' house several nights running the following week. They were beautiful light evenings now and she would cycle off there after tea as happy as a lark. They let her keep her oil paints and stuff up at the Lodge. By the weekend, it was finished and dry – a life-size copy of the Perdou painting.

When she brought it home, we all crowded round. She'd put a lot of loving care into it. It was really good. At least, that's what I thought at the time, but of course I'm no expert. To my unpractised eye it looked remarkably like the original, though even I could see that Sarah hadn't *quite* caught the subtle blues and greys of the original, nor the lovely misty quality of that long-lost chateau. All the same, I thought she'd done it well.

'I'm longing to show it to Monsieur Perdou on Monday!' she exclaimed. 'It'll be such a surprise for him. He doesn't know I've been doing it.'

On Monday evening she returned from college without the canvas. She'd set off so jauntily in the morning, but one look at her and I knew she'd suffered a disappointment.

'Didn't he like it?' I asked.

'Not much,' said Sarah ruefully. 'In fact, he criti-

45

cized it like mad. Of course he was right,' she added quickly. 'And I'm glad he was honest. There's no room for politeness when one's in pursuit of excellence! There must be integrity between tutor and student! Now I see where I went wrong. I hadn't got the basic perspective right, the texture was uneven – '

She went on at some length and in boring detail, recounting M. Perdou's criticisms.

'And where is it now?'

'Where's what?'

'Your painting, of course, Sar!' I said.

'Oh, I disposed of it at college,' she replied with disdain.

'What, chucked it away?' I asked in amazement.

'More or less,' replied Sarah. 'It was only an exercise, after all.'

Poor Sarah! But of course, one might have guessed that M. Perdou wasn't the sort to pull any punches. And besides, its shortcomings had only reminded him of the supposed perfection of the original. It was all so predictable!

'Was he ratty with you then, Sar? Wasn't he even pleased that you'd *tried* to copy it?'

'Oh, yes!' Sarah's face brightened then and she looked quite happy. 'He was secretly touched, I could tell. He gave me such a lovely smile when he'd finished tearing me into little pieces!'

'Then your idea wasn't a complete washout!' I said, in relief. 'Was it?'

'No, of course not!' Sarah shook her head vigorously. 'I was just a bit silly to think he might want to keep any feeble effort of mine. That it could *really* make up for his disappointment.' She stared into space. 'I think it was really mean of Mr Pudham,' she stated.

And that should have been the end of the story.

As term passed, the unfortunate incident of the Perdou painting scarcely entered my head again.

In any case, very soon after that poor M. Perdou went into a nursing home, under doctor's orders, to have six weeks' complete rest. A policeman had found him wandering round the silent civic centre late one night, carrying his big brief case and looking for all the world as though it were time to go to work. He'd been dazed and unable to remember what he was doing there. The policeman had taken him home and called a doctor, who at once diagnosed that M. Perdou was suffering from nervous exhaustion. The burden of family and financial worries had been too great to bear, and he had been neglecting himself and not eating or sleeping properly for some time.

'He's got to have complete bed rest!' said Sarah, coming home from college, pale with the news. 'He won't even be allowed visitors for a month. Isn't it awful.'

'It's all for the best,' said Gran. 'They'll feed him up and make a new man of him up at the Clutterhouse Clinic. It's supposed to be very good there. A friend of Mrs Hayes went in, you know, and it worked wonders for her.' Mrs Hayes was Gran's best friend in Haven and lived at Meadowlands, the old people's bungalows just near our house. 'You wait and see, Sarah, it'll be all for the best,' Gran repeated.

For once I was inclined to think Gran was right because, with hindsight, I could see that M. Perdou had been in a pretty bad way.

With M. Perdou completely off the scene for some

weeks, we rather expected his influence around the place to decline – we thought that Sarah would soon be off in pursuit of some new enthusiasm. However, apart from a brief flirtation with New Guinea primitive art after one of the boys at college took her to an exhibition in London, she remained totally loyal to her absent tutor, eating her croissants and even taking up French conversation evening classes at the college one night a week.

Sarah was very impatient to visit Monsieur Perdou, but the Clutterhouse Clinic kept putting her off. He was making slower progress than expected, it seemed. 'But I'll definitely be able to see him by half term, Jill!' she told me.

I was too busy with my own life to feel very involved in Sarah's. This was my second summer term at Haven school and I was enjoying it very much – even though you're supposed to pretend that you *don't* enjoy school much in some circles.

I was disappointed not to find my tennis improving – though it was good to see Pudding play, I must say, and each time she got through to another round of the Junior Cup, Lindy and I would go along and cheer.

But the swimming – that was another story. The school had a superb pool and a very good coach in Mr Mercer. He was nice! Both Lindy and I had a real craze on swimming that summer and by half term we were about the two best swimmers in 2N, if you didn't count Candy Morris – she was really exceptional.

'You're catching up with me!' wailed Candy one day. 'I want somebody who's faster than me so I can race against *them* and catch up with them.'

So term was passing happily, the Perdou painting all but forgotten.

At the end of May, during the half-term break, Sarah was allowed to go and visit the clinic at last. She came back in a definitely chirpy mood.

'He looks much better, Jill,' she told me, up in our bedroom. 'He's still not quite himself, and he's not allowed to leave the clinic or go on any little excursions yet. But he's allowed to sit out on the verandah and look at the grounds – they're lovely.'

'Did you talk to him in French?'

'Yes!' said Sarah. She smiled and looked dreamy. 'I made tons of mistakes and he kept having to correct me, but he was laughing about it – not at all ratty! I'm sure he'll be well enough to come back to college next term. I just didn't realize before how ratty he was getting, none of us did. It was because he was so dreadfully ill, and none of us realized. It's funny, Jill, but there's something different about him now – he seems, well, *serene*, almost. And do you know what?'

'What?' I asked politely, glancing at the clock. I was supposed to be cycling down to the river with Lindy in a few minutes' time.

'He's totally accepted that business of Mr Pudham owning his great-grandfather's painting. He says he's ashamed for not counting his blessings – the miracle of having found a Perdou painting at last, to be living in the very town where it's housed! Actually he told me that he's just living for the moment when he can go and look at it again, when he's better. Do you think the Pudhams will mind?'

'Oh, I'm sure they won't,' I said with relief.

'He really accepts the situation now, Jill, so you don't need to feel guilty any more. It's made him happy after all.'

'Good!' I said, with real feeling. 'I'm glad!'

I didn't think that Mr Pudham would be one to hold a grudge, especially as he knew about M. Perdou's illness. He'd even asked after him once when I'd met him in the town. I was sure fences would soon be mended and that the Frenchman, once better, would be welcome at Les-Jen Lodge to look at the painting now and then, as long as there was no longer any likelihood of a scene. Surely the Pudhams wouldn't be unfriendly?

The very same weekend came proof that my hunch was right.

Pudding rang our house on the Saturday afternoon.

'Daddy's having a cocktail party this evening, Jill, and he wondered if your sister would like to come. It's to do with the foundation stone being laid for the first factory, but the architect's coming – and – well, Daddy's going to hang that painting in the drawing room just for his benefit.'

Even after all this time, Pudding squirmed a little at having to mention the Perdou painting.

'Why does your Dad want Sarah to come?' I asked with interest.

'Well Mr Primrose, that's the architect, happens to be a real expert on French Impressionist painting and he'll probably be able to value the picture for Daddy. Daddy thought Sarah might like to be there and then she might have something exciting to tell Monsieur Perdou when she goes to visit him.'

'Exciting?'

'What I mean is, Jill, it's probably worth quite a bit and Daddy hopes it'll make Monsieur Perdou feel better – about why he couldn't sell it to him – and also make him feel good that his ancestor's on the up and up.'

'Monsieur Perdou doesn't mind about your Dad not selling any more,' I explained. 'He's got over that now. But, yes, I bet he'd love to know how much it's worth – I'll tell Sarah about the party the minute she comes in. She's out shopping with Roy.'

Roy Brewster, who helped to run the youth club that Lindy and I belonged to, was my sister's steady boy friend.

Sarah went to the cocktail party, of course. Just try keeping my sister away from a party! I was out of the house when she left at about six o' clock but Dad, who drove her there, said she looked very nice.

She was gone a long time for a cocktail party that was only supposed to last a couple of hours, because it was past nine o' clock when I heard the Pudhams' car stop outside and then drive off.

'Hi, Sarah!' I said, peering over the banister into the hall as she came in through the front door. 'Had a good time?'

'Shut up, Jill!' snapped Sarah, rushing straight past me and up the stairs to our bedroom. Her cheeks looked tear-stained. 'Of course I didn't!'

What on earth could have happened at Les-Jen Lodge?

51

7

❀ ❀ ❀

Pudding is Peculiar

'Sarah!'

I stood at the bottom of the stairs at home, gazing upwards in astonishment as I heard her crash across the landing in the direction of our big bedroom.

'Sarah – ?' I called again. But my voice trailed away, helplessly, as I heard the door slam behind her upstairs.

'Was that Sarah back?' asked Gran then, suddenly putting her head out of the kitchen, a drying-up cloth in her hand. 'Did she have a lovely time?'

'Dunno, Gran,' I said. I walked slowly into the kitchen, feeling uneasy, took the cloth from Gran and started polishing up a casserole dish that had been too awkward to go in the dishwasher. 'I'll do this.'

Mum, Dad and Tony had gone to see a film.

'Perhaps she wants supper?' Gran said brightly. She bustled over to the oven. 'Shall I heat up the rest of the pie? What do you think, Jill?'

'I – er – ' As Gran's words sank in, I quickly shook my head. 'No, I'm sure Sarah doesn't want any supper. I mean – she's gone straight up to the bedroom. She'd have said if she'd wanted any.'

'Up to your room? But it's nowhere near her bedtime.'

'Oh, don't fuss, Gran,' I said hurriedly, anxious not to let her suspect there might be something the matter. 'She's probably had too much to – ' I was going to say 'drink' but quickly changed my mind – 'too much holiday work, Gran. Gone up to finish off her sketches, maybe.'

'Ah yes,' Gran chuckled to herself, quite satisfied now. 'She's the artist, our Sarah. Always was. I remember saying to Henry when she was just a little girl: "Mark my words, Henry, little Sarah's going to be an artist one day." She was always crayoning away. I don't expect you remember that, Jill. You were just a baby then. I'm so pleased she's getting on nicely at the college. Mind you,' she spoke confidentially, 'I don't think your father's got a lot of patience with it. But I'm on Sarah's side, Jill. She'll get herself into the Royal Academy one of these fine days. Oh, yes, I'm on Sarah's side. Let me tell you, it runs in the family. My great-aunt on my mother's side did the most beautiful water colours . . .'

Gran was on one of her pet themes now, and she expounded it at considerable length, but I found it difficult to listen to her. I kept thinking about Sarah and wondering what had happened to upset her so much.

As soon as Gran had settled down in front of the television I took my courage in both hands and marched straight up to our room and in through the door.

'Go away, Jill!' came a muffled voice.

'Whatever's wrong, Sar?' I said. 'Honestly, you *must* tell me.'

She'd been lying face downwards on her bed, her face buried in the pillow. Now she sat up and wiped

53

her sleeve across her eyes as though to wipe some tears away. Then she blinked at me, rather crossly.

'You should have knocked, Jill,' she said, resentfully.

'I live here, too!' I exclaimed. 'Besides, something's happened. You're crying!'

'Crying?' she snapped back at me. 'Of course I'm not crying.'

If Sarah could have seen her face in the mirror at that moment, she'd have realized how comical her words sounded. But I was rather taken aback. I didn't often see her like this – on the defensive. Unapproachable.

'But there is *something* the matter?' I said, rather lamely.

'Do stop it, Jill.' She had her emotions under control now. 'Stop asking me silly questions. Nothing's the matter. I'm just rather – rather depressed this evening. I expect it was the wine. You know I'm not used to drinking wine. That's all. I want to be left alone.' She waved a hand towards the door. 'Off you go. Let me get ready to have a bath. I need an early night.'

Chastened, I went downstairs then and joined Gran in front of the television set.

Chastened – and deeply mystified.

'I'm going to cross-question Pudding about it as soon as I get a chance to, at school! Yes, that's what I'll do. I'll question her! *She* must know what happened at her house on Saturday evening! I've *got* to get to the bottom of this mystery.'

My thoughts were churning over and over as fast as the pedals of my bike.

It was Monday morning and I was cycling to school.

There was a summery smell in the air – the trees in the avenues of Haven were fully in leaf now, the front gardens beginning to burgeon. The sun was coming up and we were sure to have swimming today. I should have felt at peace with the world, but the very pleasantness of the day just reminded me how worried I was – the way it can, sometimes.

I was now certain there was a very big mystery afoot. At breakfast, Sarah had been silent and dejected, not her usual self at all. We'd scarcely been able to get a civil word out of her. And instead of rushing round and getting ready for college immediately after breakfast, as she usually did, she'd been mooning around and dragging her feet when I left for school – as though she didn't much want to go.

She'd spent most of Sunday with Roy, who'd now gone off for a week's course in Birmingham to do with his job. But I was sure it couldn't be that which had depressed her. He was only going for a week!

'What *can* have happened?' I wondered for the tenth time. 'It's obvious that Sar's not going to talk about it. Surely Pudding will give me a clue! Did Sar have a row with her Dad on Saturday night?'

But why? What about? Pudding would tell me!

I'd been longing to phone her all day Sunday, but I hadn't dared, not with our phone being in the hall and the family's flapping ears all around.

At school that day came my next big shock.

From the moment I saw Pudding, I knew that something was wrong. I'd decided not to charge at the mystery like a bull at a gate, but just to ease the conversation round to it gently. So I walked into 2N before lessons began, and sauntered up to Pudding, who was sorting out the books in her desk.

'Hi, Pud,' I said nonchalantly. 'Isn't it this week you've got to play Donna Watson?' – and cheerfully clapped her on the shoulder.

She jumped!

She actually shrank away from me for a moment, and from the look on her face you'd have thought I'd said: 'By the way I've got the plague!' or 'Don't look now, but I've had a head transplant!' instead of what I'd actually said.

Then she went bright red, refused to meet my eye and just stared down into her desk, fumbling with the books there.

'What's the matter with *you*?' I asked, falteringly.

'Sorry, Jill.' She went on staring down at her books. 'You made me jump, that's all, suddenly appearing like that.'

'Well – ' I tried to make her laugh, though I felt distinctly uneasy – 'I haven't left the school, you know. I'm still here.' I came and gazed at the books in her desk. 'Mmmm. Fascinating,' I joked. 'Heron & Black's Atlas, Thomson's Intermediate Biology and . . . oooh!' I snatched up one of the books. 'Armstrong's Algebra – what a blockbuster! No wonder you can't take your eyes off it!'

At last Pudding looked up from her open desk and smiled. It was a sheepish smile, though. She was embarrassed to see me, all right.

She *knew* something! There was no point in beating about the bush.

'Look,' I said awkwardly, 'what's the matter?' I glanced round, anxious that no one should overhear us. 'Why are you so embarrassed? What's happened?'

She looked down once more and whispered in despair: 'Jill! Don't you know?'

56

'I know it's to do with Sarah,' I said, bluffing quickly. 'Saturday night.'

'But she hasn't told you?'

My heart missed a beat.

'She hasn't told me anything,' I said then. 'But you can.'

'No, Jill!' she said fiercely. She looked very stubborn. 'I can't tell you anything. Not without Sarah's permission. She's the only one who can tell you and she probably won't!'

She turned her back on me then, presenting an impenetrable wall. Moments later Miss Rawlings came in, and then hordes of our classmates to dump their books before assembly.

Twice more that day I tried to question Pudding, but I had no success at all. She was very tight-lipped and she seemed upset, too.

'No, Jill,' she said. 'Please don't ask me. I can't tell you.'

Lindy wondered what on earth was going on.

'Something's happened and I don't know what,' I explained as we walked across to computer studies together. 'Over the weekend. Between my sister and the Pudham family. Extraordinary! And whatever it is, there's a conspiracy of silence! Both sides. Sarah won't talk. Pudding won't talk. Deadlock!'

'We'll have to get to the bottom of it, Jill,' said Lindy.

I realized something else. Whatever it was that had happened, it had affected my friendship with Pudding. Although she tried not to show it, although she was trying to be as normal towards me as possible, she didn't feel at ease in my company any longer. I could tell.

57

'Whatever it is that Sarah's supposed to have done,' I said to Lindy, 'it's definitely making Pudding a bit peculiar.'

'So what's new?' said Lindy, who was sometimes slightly put out by my new friendship. 'She's a bit peculiar already!'

It was all very well for Lindy to joke. I felt rather hurt about the whole thing.

8

✿✿✿

The Mystery Deepens

'What classes have you got this morning, Sarah?'
Mum enquired brightly at breakfast. 'Anything interesting?'

We all glanced at Sarah. She'd been sitting there
staring dreamily into space – completely detached
from the rest of us, somehow. It was now Friday and
she'd been like this all week. I knew that Mum was
worried about her, and as usual was trying to draw her
into conversation.

'Classes?'

Sarah blinked as though suddenly waking up from
sleep, then quickly smiled and met Mum's eye.

'Let's see . . . it's Still Life on Fridays.'

'Oh, you like that, don't you!' commented Gran.

Sarah mumbled a reply and then, gazing down into
her coffee cup, she lapsed back into dreaminess.

Heavy silence . . . broken by Dad.

'Strikes me this arty-crafty way of life may not be
the ideal thing for you, my girl. You've been looking
thoroughly washed-out lately. How much are you
learning there, that's what I'd like to know? I've said
from the beginning that you might be better suited
getting a job again. You can always study art in your
spare time, if you're really interested in it.'

'Of course I'm interested in it, Dad!' Sarah flared

up, suddenly jerked out of her reverie. 'I've learnt a tremendous amount at college – a fantastic amount. I was just an ignoramus before I went there. I thought I knew a lot about drawing and I didn't know a thing. It's really worthwhile! I *love* it there . . . and . . .'

Sarah's new-found animation suddenly deserted her. Her voice trailed away to nothing. She swallowed with difficulty and Tony and I exchanged dismayed looks as we saw tears starting to well up in her eyes.

'I'm going!' she said hurriedly. She jumped up from the table and turned away from us all, obviously hoping that no one would see how upset she was. ' 'Scuse me. Got to get going. Mustn't be late, must I?'

Two minutes later we heard the front door slam.

'You shouldn't have upset her,' Mum said quietly to Dad. 'You know we've agreed to Sarah doing this course. It's not fair to keep on at her!'

'Well, I'm worried about her,' Dad confessed. 'I don't care what she says, I've got a feeling that her studies aren't going at all well.'

With that pronouncement, he got up from the table himself.

'D'you think it's because she's crazy about that French bloke?' Tony whispered to me as we went into the hall to get our stuff for school. 'D'you think she's miserable because they're still keeping him in that nursing home place?'

I shrugged.

'Search me,' I said.

Secretly, I was beginning to feel desperately worried about Sarah. She'd been completely withdrawn all week. We usually gossiped quite a lot around the place, sometimes even in our room at night, long after I was supposed to be asleep.

But all this week Sarah had been going upstairs before *me*, and – even more amazing – I'd been finding her fast asleep with the bedclothes pulled up over her head when I went to bed. Of course, Roy was away all week, but that had never had such an effect on her before.

I was convinced that it was something to do with M. Perdou all right, but not in the way Tony was suggesting. On the Wednesday I'd tried to raise the subject of the cocktail party again, asking Sarah what Mr Pudham's architect friend had valued the Perdou painting at.

'I don't know and I don't care, Jill!' Sarah had snapped at me.

Tony went off to school on this Friday morning before me – I was still trying to stuff everything in my school bag. I noticed I had two novels of Sarah's that I'd borrowed. I'd read them now, and I didn't have room for them any more.

'I'd better put them back while I remember!' I decided.

I hurried upstairs to our room and stooped down to put the books in her bookcase. I heard Mum shouting downstairs that I'd be late, so straightened up abruptly, and – crash! My shoulder caught the edge of Sarah's cupboard door, just alongside her bookcase.

It must have been ready to burst open. The door was obviously bulging and under strain because there was so much stuff packed inside the cupboard.

Now – whoosh! The contents of the cupboard cascaded down like the Niagara Falls on to the floor at my feet.

'Bother!' I said out loud. As if I wasn't late enough already!

I bent down again and started to collect up all Sarah's stuff. Only then did I realize what the things were.

I stared in astonishment.

What could this mean?

Bewildered, I stacked the things back into the cupboard, one by one.

Two art smocks, with Sarah's name tapes sewn on them. Paints, paintbrushes, palettes, a drawing board – all marked *Sarah Robinson*. And three enormous folios, containing paintings and drawings with marks and comments on them: Sarah's college work.

'All Sarah's term-time things,' I mused, frowning hard. 'The things she normally keeps up at college. She *needs* them. She uses them every day, doesn't she? So what are they doing here for goodness' sake? Why's she brought them back and stuffed them away in a cupboard?'

With the things safely inside once more, I carefully rammed the cupboard door firmly shut. Then I tiptoed furtively out of our bedroom. My heart was pounding and I felt guilty. I knew that I'd seen something I wasn't meant to see.

I left the house and cycled slowly down the road. I was getting towards being late for school now, but somehow I couldn't go straight there. My thoughts were in too much of a turmoil. I couldn't stop thinking about my sister.

'There's something terribly funny going on,' I thought. 'It's all to do with that evening at Les-Jen Lodge. Sarah's in real trouble – maybe much more than I thought.'

My mind shied away from thinking it through any further. At that moment, I had just one simple burning objective – to find Sarah and have a show-down about the mystery!

'Whatever trouble she's in, she's just *got* to share it with someone,' I told myself. 'She can't go on facing it alone like this. It's not even as if she's got Roy to talk to this week.'

I cycled round the streets of Haven for some time – and then at last I caught sight of her! Even viewed from the back – and from a distance – her startlingly bright outfit was unmistakable.

She was walking along very slowly, like someone in a dream. She was going in quite the wrong direction for Haven college.

She was heading, in fact, for the main gates of Pettigrew Park. Strolling along, as though she had all the time in the world.

Perhaps she had.

I got off my bike and wheeled it along the pave-ment, following Sarah at a cautious distance. As I entered the park and dumped the bike beside some rhododendron bushes, a group of fighting sparrows flurried out of my way.

I tip-toed along the path and reached the end of the shrubbery, then peered out. I could see Sarah quite clearly. She was sitting on one of the green park seats, on her own, beneath a dripping oak tree. It had rained in the night and the day was now dull, the sky grey and overcast.

She'd taken a book out of her pocket and was reading it. The park was empty at this time of the morning, apart from an elderly woman walking her dog in the distance, and my sister looked a lonely figure, just sitting there on the park seat, reading.

'Well.' I swallowed hard. 'Here goes.'

I ran across the wet grass. Sarah didn't notice me until I was within a few yards of her. She looked up from her book, her eyes wide and startled.

'Jill! What are you doing here?'

'I followed you,' I said flatly.

'What a nerve!' she flared up.

'Why aren't you at college? What about your classes? I thought you were getting there early?'

Sarah blushed red.

'I . . . I . . .' She tried to hide her paperback, a book of Victorian poetry. 'I just changed my mind, that's all. I just decided, well, to give it a miss this morning – '

'*Just* this morning?' I asked. I blurted it out: 'All your college stuff's in the cupboard at home!'

She knew then that her secret was out.

'Oh, Jill.' She stared at me, dumbfounded. Then she was biting her lip, fighting back the tears. 'Oh . . . Jill . . .'

She buried her face in her hands and sobbed.

'You might as well know, then. Only Mum and Dad mustn't find out. If you tell them, I'll kill you! I – I've been . . .' She could hardly bring herself to say it. 'I've been suspended!'

'Sar! You haven't?!'

From the moment I'd seen her things in the cupboard at home, I'd suspected it – but, even hearing her say the word, I could only just bring myself to believe it.

'Since when?'

She stopped crying then and raised her tear-stained face, looking ashamed.

64

'Since Monday!' she replied.

I sank down on to the park seat, alongside her.

'Oh, Sar!' My own eyes felt watery now. 'You mean you've been doing this since Monday, coming to the park every day? Killing time . . . pretending you're still at college? So no one would know?'

'They're not going to know!' Sarah repeated, fiercely. She fixed her eyes on me. 'I mean that, Jill! There's no reason why they should. I couldn't bear it if Mum and Dad found out. You know how Dad's been against me going to college from the start. But there's someone else who mustn't find out. Someone I think the world of.'

Monsieur Perdou?

'But they'll all *have* to know sooner or later.'

'No!' Sarah exclaimed. 'Very soon, Mr Williams will find out I didn't do it. Then he'll take me back at college! And no one'll ever be any the wiser.'

Suddenly I felt cold, and shivered.

'Find out you didn't do *what*, Sar?' I whispered. The elderly lady with her dog was passing right by us. 'What are you supposed to have done?'

9

❀ ❀ ❀

Inquiries

We sat together on the seat in silence, waiting for the old lady to pass out of earshot. It was a grey morning in Pettigrew Park, and getting greyer. I don't know if it was just the weather that was making me shiver, or the scared feeling in the pit of my stomach.

'Come on, Spot!'

With a last friendly snuffle round our feet the little dog ran off in pursuit of his owner, and we were alone again.

'Find out that you didn't do *what*, Sar?' I repeated.

At last Sarah spoke. She'd been staring into space.

'I can't tell you, Jill,' she said simply. 'It – it's too complicated.'

'It's something to do with the Pudhams, isn't it?' I persisted. 'Was it them who got you into trouble?'

'I suppose you could put it that way.'

'Pudding knows all about it, doesn't she?' I went on. I had to try and get through that brick wall somehow! 'She's been funny towards me at school this week. Sort of embarrassed. I *knew* something had happened. But she won't talk about it, either. Not without your permission. Come on, you've *got* to tell me!'

'No!' Sarah said. Her lip trembled and she looked at me sympathetically. 'Oh, poor Jill. But I don't want to

66

talk about it. Can't you see that?' She grabbed hold of my wrist and showed me my watch: 'Look at the time – you're late for school. Hours late. You'd better get going.'

'I'm not going. Not until you tell me.'

'Ask Pudding – or whatever her ridiculous name is,' Sarah replied. 'Go on Jill – ask her, when you get to school. You have my permission. Here . . .'

She took a pencil and notepad out of her pocket, scribbled something, and then ripped off the page and handed it to me.

'Here you are. You can give it to her. My written permission.'

I stood up and took the note, in silence. This was Sarah at her most stubborn. She wasn't going to talk. And it was true enough that I was late for school – very late! In a way, her attitude hurt me. But I think she was trying to tell me something. She'd find it much easier if I heard the story from someone else. That was all.

'One more thing, Jill,' said Sarah as I turned to go. She seemed very concerned. 'Swear you won't tell *anyone* that I've been suspended. They mustn't find out at home. They've got to go on thinking I'm at college. Dad would go straight to see . . .'

'Not even Lindy?' I said.

'You can tell Lindy. No one else.'

'I think you're mad,' I murmured. 'But – all right. If it makes you any happier, then I swear.'

I walked away across the smooth grass. When I reached the path through the shrubbery, I glanced back. Sarah was once more buried in her book, a solitary figure on the park seat. I thought of the empty day stretching ahead of her.

67

'You'd better talk now, Polly Pudham, or else!' I thought to myself as I pedalled furiously all the way to school.

'All right, Jill. Seeing she's given her permission. I – I'll tell you. Don't know why she couldn't tell you herself, though.'

I'd been so late for school that I'd missed assembly altogether, but had scrambled into 2N just in time for register. Straight afterwards I cornered Pudding, before she could escape. She was on her way to French and we were in different divisions. I caught hold of her arm, and pulled her along the corridor and round the corner, out of sight. 'Listen, Pudding, this is urgent!' I'd said, and handed her Sarah's note. Now her face was red and embarrassed.

She said: 'Remember the Perdou painting? Remember your sister painted a copy of it?'

The Perdou painting! I felt uneasy stirrings.

'What about it?' I said. My hands felt rather clammy.

'Well, remember Daddy's cocktail party last Saturday? Remember this man was there – Daddy's architect!' Pudding was starting to gabble. 'Well, remember Daddy was going to get him to value the Perdou painting? Daddy wanted to hang on to that painting, you know.'

'Yes, yes,' I nodded, uneasily. Why was she looking reproachful and speaking in the past tense?

'Well.' Pudding gulped. 'Mr Primrose looked at it and just laughed. He said it wasn't an old painting at all. Probably done in the last three months! The canvas was new. So was the paint. Probably done by an art student. Just a copy.'

A chill ran down my spine.

'Sarah's copy?'

'Yes.' Pudding stared down at the floor, too upset to meet my eyes. 'It was Sarah's copy all right. Daddy summoned her to his study, straight after the party. He showed her the painting and she admitted it was that copy she'd made, you know, a few weeks ago. You see what must have happened, Jill?' Pudding turned away. 'Some time in the past few weeks she must have sneaked into our house, taken the Perdou painting out of the frame and replaced it with her copy.'

'What?' I gasped. 'Sarah *admitted that*?'

'No! She didn't exactly admit it. She told Daddy some story about throwing the copy away. But, I ask you. Is that likely?'

'Yes!' I said furiously. 'If she says so!' I was beginning to feel sick. 'So you think my sister stole the genuine painting – and replaced it with her copy? *You think Sarah's a thief*?'

'I . . . I . . .' Pudding looked quite scared of me. 'Jill – I'm supposed to be at French! I don't know what to believe. Why did she want to make the copy in the first place? It was a weird thing to do, just for no reason. And if she *did* throw the copy away afterwards, who found it? And how could they possibly have known that it was a copy of *Le Chateau Perdou* and the original was hanging in our house?'

'I expect your mother broadcast it all over Haven – ' I began scornfully, but Pudding cut me off.

'Only Sarah knew. And Sarah fell in love with the painting, from the moment she saw it. She probably thought Daddy didn't really appreciate it! That he wouldn't even notice if it went, and a copy hung there in its place! And,' she spread out her hands ruefully,

69

'let's face it, Jill. She was quite right! He didn't appreciate it. He didn't notice a jot of difference! None of us did. It was only this man coming and – '

'Shut up!' I mouthed at her furiously. I grabbed her shoulders and shook her, I was so angry. 'How dare you say my sister's a thief, just because the evidence is against her! If she says she threw away the copy, then she *did*. She told me so at the time! Someone else must have got hold of it – '

Pudding looked on the verge of tears.

'We're supposed to be at French! If you must know, I did your sister a good turn. Daddy was all set to go to the police! I begged him – pleaded with him – not to. It's only thanks to me he didn't. And – ' she paused – 'I did it because we're friends, Jill.'

'But he told them about it at college?'

'Yes – he rang the principal on Monday. He told Sarah he would. He had to do that. He feels it's very bad that someone should be getting art instruction at the taxpayers' expense and then putting their talents to a dishonest purpose.'

I was speechless as Pudding babbled on.

'But Daddy played the whole thing down – because I begged him to. He told the principal that he would leave it to him to take the necessary disciplinary action – and also to see to it that the painting was restored to its rightful owner as soon as possible. And that would be the end of the matter.'

A picture of Sarah flashed into my mind; sitting in the park all alone, too scared to let the family know what had happened.

'Thanks for believing the worst of my sister!' I said, as she hurried off. I felt really spiteful. 'With friends like you, who needs enemies?'

70

She turned and looked at me. 'Daddy's still waiting to get his painting back,' she said meaningfully. Then she disappeared round the corner, out of sight.

For the rest of the day we didn't speak to each other. And I couldn't bring myself to tell Lindy about it, either, even if she was my best friend. Not until I'd spoken to Sarah again.

'What *can* I do, Jill?' sighed Sarah. 'Do let's stop talking about it, please. I'm fed up with the subject. You know what's happened. Surely you're satisfied now.'

We were sitting on the sofa in the hall after tea. I got the feeling that Sarah was hoping the phone would ring. She kept glancing towards it.

'Satisfied?' I whispered. 'Honestly, you are hopeless. How can you just sit there and vaguely hope that everything will turn out right!'

'But it will, Jill! I know it will!' she said, keeping her voice low. 'I didn't pinch the wretched painting. I laughed in Mr Williams's face when he suggested it – in fact I was pretty rude to him. I think that's the real reason he suspended me. But he said it was only until he'd made inquiries. He said he'd be making a few inquiries this week. I'll be cleared soon, and then I can go back to college!'

She studied her finger-nails before going to work on them with some new varnish.

'Until that happens, until things turn out right, I just have to lie low and keep up this pretence with Mum and Dad. *They* mustn't know what's happened. Remember, you *promised*.'

71

I nodded miserably – but Sarah suddenly jumped up. The phone was ringing.

'Hurray!' she said, eyes shining. 'Mr Williams said he'd ring me at the end of the week. Perhaps that's him now!'

She picked up the phone, and when I heard her say 'Sarah Robinson *speaking*' I knew it must be the expected call. I hurriedly went through into the lounge and shut the door, to leave her in peace.

'Hallo, Jill,' said Gran. I then proceeded to conduct a loud conversation with her, just to make sure there was no danger of Sarah's conversation in the hall being overheard.

Then – ding! That was the receiver being replaced. Conversation over. How had it gone?

What had been the result of the principal's inquiries? They'd taken long enough! Was Sarah right to be optimistic, I wondered?

Then – slam. That was the front door! Quickly I glanced through our big windows. Sarah was marching off down the garden path, head in the air. I got the feeling she was in a rage!

'Where are you off to now, Jill?'

'Just going to ask Sarah to get me something, Gran!' I said quickly.

I caught up with Sarah halfway down the road.

'Where are you off to?' I fell into step beside her. She looked white.

'Nowhere in particular. I've got a splitting headache.'

'Was that Mr Williams? Has he made inquiries? What did he say?'

'Do you really want to know?' she said. Then: 'One of the boys saw Blakey with my painting, he remembered seeing him with it. Taking it over to his bungalow.'

'Who's Blakey?'

'Mr Blake. The caretaker up at college. He's sweet.'

'Then you're in the clear – !' I began excitedly.

'Are you joking?' said Sarah. She frowned and looked very bewildered.

We had reached the top end of Newlands Park, the cul-de-sac end where the footpath leads through to the north-east Community Centre. There was a stone pillar at the entrance to the public footpath, to discourage people from riding their bikes through there. Sarah had now stopped dead and put both hands on top of the pillar, leaning against it as though she needed its support. She was still very pale, and she spoke slowly and carefully, with disbelief – as though it were all a bad dream.

'The principal questioned Blakey. He'd found my picture when he cleared out – it was with a pile of rubbish outside the art room. That's where I put it, I remember now. Well, apparently Blakey liked it and took it back to the bungalow. But he hasn't got it now.'

'Who has?'

'According to Blakey somebody took it away!' said Sarah. 'That's what he told the principal. I don't know whether he knows *who* or not. Mr Williams isn't saying. He just says he's going to make further inquiries next week, and in the meantime my suspension stays. So I'm still under suspicion, it seems!'

What a dramatic turn of events! What was Sarah looking so upset about? I grabbed her arm, excitedly.

'Pudding thought she was doing you a good turn, stopping her father from going to the police! I never thought it was such a good idea! Will Mr Williams go to the police now?'

'Of course he won't, Jill. He doesn't want the good name of the college involved in any scandal – '

'But if this Mr Blake is lying to him – then it's obvious that *he's* the person who broke into Les-Jen Lodge and switched your picture with the real Perdou painting.'

'He doesn't think Blakey is lying,' said Sarah, in a deadpan voice. 'I can tell he doesn't. And if you knew Blakey, you'd know he's not the lying sort. No, Mr Williams is tending to think that I've pinched the painting and he's given me a last chance to own up and produce it. He didn't say so, not in so many words. But it was all there in his tone of voice.'

I let go of her arm and turned away from her, feeling very angry. Why was Sarah being so *wet* about it all?

'Where are you going, Jill?' she asked in alarm.

'I'm going home to tell Dad!' I exclaimed. 'Dad'll call the police. He won't stand for this! He won't stand for having you under suspicion like this! What grounds have they got?'

She stood there, thunderstruck, as I walked away.

Halfway back along the road I heard racing footsteps behind me.

'Jill!' cried Sarah in anguish.

She caught hold of my arm and physically restrained me.

'Please don't tell Dad. Once the police are brought in the whole thing will be all over Haven. It's been kept hush-hush so far and that's the way I want it!'

'*Why*?'

'Because of Monsieur Perdou, of course,' she said, with great feeling. 'He thinks his great-grandad's

74

painting is safe here in Haven – hanging up on the wall of the back lobby at Les-Jen Lodge. He's just living for the moment when he'll be fit and well again and can get out and about – well enough to go and look at it, touch it, let his eyes linger upon it. He loves that painting. It's part of him, like a child. Maybe he even daydreams of having enough money one day to tempt Mr Pudham to sell it, I don't know.'

'But that's not a good enough reason for you to go through all this,' I protested.

'Oh yes it is,' she said, her lips set in a firm line. 'If he were to get to hear that the painting's gone – been stolen – vanished without a trace and is maybe a million miles away by now . . . Well, it could *kill* him, Jill! You know the doctors are worried about him. Do you want to have that on your conscience?'

I fell silent and stared down at the pavement, miserably.

'So you won't tell Dad, will you, Jill? Not yet. Not this weekend. Promise?'

So I promised. And went straight back indoors to phone Lindy. Leaving Sarah to walk the streets and, I hoped, get rid of her headache.

In the meantime Lindy might have some ideas. Maybe she would know the best thing to do.

10

❀❀❀

The Two Investigators

'Listen, Lindy. Sarah's in dreadful trouble.' I had to
keep my voice low, so that the family wouldn't hear.
'She's too wet and feeble to help herself. She won't let
me tell Dad and . . . well, anyway, we've got to try
and do something without *her*.'

'Is it to do with that party at the Pudhams? Is it?
Jill! Tell all!'

'Can't talk here. Meet you in Cobbers in half an
hour. Bring your bike!'

We arrived at our favourite coffee bar at exactly the
same time.

'Hi, Jill!' Lindy's green eyes were sparkling with
interest. Her curly hair was windblown.

For the first time in days, I felt optimistic. It would
be a relief to tell Lindy everything at last.

'Hi, Lindy! Hope you didn't mind my dragging you
out. Didn't dare talk on the phone! You see, none of
the family knows about it – about Sarah.'

'Sounds very mysterious,' said Lindy. 'Come on –
tell me!'

'Let's go inside.'

We settled down in a private alcove just inside
Cobbers, near the door, and ordered hot chocolate.

Then, haltingly, I brought Lindy right up to date
with the whole story. When I'd finished, she just
gazed at me – her eyes wide with horror.

'It's ridiculous! The idea of Sarah . . . the idea of her *stealing*. Taking that picture from the Pudhams' house and replacing it with that copy she painted. I just don't believe it! Your sister just isn't the type! Why doesn't the head of the college just take her word for it? He must be a complete idiot and fool!'

'I gather she told him something like that, and that's one of the reasons she's been suspended,' I said, ruefully. But I gazed gratefully at Lindy. 'Oh, it's such a relief to know you feel just the same way about it as I do.'

I glanced at Lindy and automatically lowered my voice:

'Pudding thinks the worst of Sarah. She thinks she's guilty. I can tell – the way she's so embarrassed with me! It's really hurtful.'

'Oh, she would,' said Lindy scornfully, still slightly jealous of Pudding. 'But then, after all,' she said more reasonably, 'the painting's been pinched from *her* parents, so it's probably difficult for her to see the whole thing objectively.'

'I must say she's tried to help,' I said. 'It's only thanks to her begging him not to that her father didn't go to the police and make a scandal. But she still assumes Sarah *is* guilty, and that's what really annoys me. I wish her Dad *had* gone to the police!' I added, with feeling. 'Then the whole thing might have been cleared up by now. Whatever Sarah says about poor old Monsieur Perdou.'

'And let's face it, Jill,' said Lindy. 'Mr Pudham may not have gone to the police – but he's got Sarah into big trouble at college. And it's all based on circumstantial evidence!'

Lindy enjoyed saying that. Lately she'd borrowed a

book on famous trials from the public library and had confided to me that she now wanted to be a lawyer when she grew up.

'There's only one piece of *actual* evidence,' she pointed out. 'And that's the Perdou painting. But where is it? It's vanished! Find that, and we're halfway to finding the thief!'

'And what's Sarah doing to try and prove her innocence?' I complained. 'Absolutely *nothing*! She's being so feeble – just vaguely hoping that things will turn out right when Mr Williams has made some more inquiries.'

'I expect she feels rather stunned by it all,' said Lindy. 'I know I would be. That's where we come in, Jill. If she won't help herself, then we've got to help her!' A business-like gleam came into her eyes. 'We've got to try and track down this stolen painting. At least we can try! Either the caretaker's telling lies and has flogged it, or else somebody at the college really *did* pinch Sarah's copy from his bungalow – I mean they have got a few weird characters there, haven't they – made the switch and then flogged the original. It might still be in the town! Now, Jill, where would you go if you wanted to sell a painting quickly?'

I was beginning to feel excited – this was like being a proper investigator.

'Well, there's Johnny's Junk Shop for a start!' I exclaimed. 'That's full of bits and pieces and Mum says they're all over-priced.'

'What about that man who sets up his antique stall in the market on Saturday mornings?' Lindy exclaimed. 'He looks really shady – he looks the sort who'd buy something without asking too many questions about where it's come from!'

'Let's meet up first thing tomorrow morning then,' I suggested. 'We can scour the likeliest shops and if we draw a blank there we can try the market. Isn't it lucky it's Saturday tomorrow!'

When we parted that evening Lindy frowned at me and said:

'Jill, why on earth did you ask me to bring my bike? It would have been quicker to walk.'

'It doesn't matter now,' I said. 'Let's try this other plan instead.'

'What will you give me for this very fine water colour? Am I bid ten pounds? Who'll bid me ten pounds? Come on, ladies and gentlemen. Shall we start the bidding at ten pounds?'

In the crowded auction room, a hand went up – then another – and another.

'Fifteen – '

'Sixteen – '

'Any advance on sixteen pounds, ladies and gentlemen? No advance on sixteen? Going at sixteen. Going . . . going . . . GONE.'

The lady in the red coat who'd bid successfully for the water colour smiled in triumph, to have beaten her rivals. But Lindy and I merely exchanged rueful, weary glances.

We'd arrived at the auction puffed out and had bagged the best seats in the saleroom, right near the front. We'd drawn a blank at the junk shops and in the market too, so it seemed like fate when we'd seen the poster announcing a Fine Art Sale at Haven Auction Rooms, starting at 11 a.m. prompt. We'd run all the way and had arrived just as it started. Luckily the paintings were the first fifty lots – with porcelain and silver to follow later.

Since nine o'clock that morning when the shops had opened we'd been shown dozens of paintings, but of *the* painting, *Le Chateau Perdou*, there hadn't been a sign, a trace or a glimmer. It had all been very wearying and disheartening.

It had given us a last ray of hope, this auction. But now our hopes were sinking again, fast. What a waste of time! We'd been sitting there for over an hour, watching one painting after another come under the auctioneer's hammer. Big paintings, little paintings, good ones, bad ones . . . but nothing that remotely resembled the Perdou painting which mattered so desperately!

'And now, ladies and gentlemen, the last of the pictures. Lot number fifty. Two very fine Victorian etchings. Shall we start the bidding at thirty pounds? Who will bid me thirty pounds for these very fine Victorian etchings?'

Lindy nudged me.

'Come on, Jill.' Her voice was thick with disappointment. 'We might as well go.'

We got up as quietly as possible and tip-toed out of the crowded saleroom, while the bidding for the etchings grew more and more exciting.

'Forty-five . . .'

'Fifty!'

The doorman gave us a rather odd look as we went out into the street. We were wearing our scruffiest clothes and had got filthy sorting through old furniture and junk shops. We probably looked as though we couldn't raise fifty pence between us, let alone fifty pounds.

80

'Well . . .' Lindy kicked a small stone, sending it rattling along the pavement. 'That seems to be that. We'd better get our bikes. Oh, Jill, isn't it *hopeless*? I suppose the missing painting must be miles away by now. Probably sitting in London in the National Gallery or somewhere!'

I swallowed hard. It looked like we'd have to try my idea, after all!

'There's just one last thing we can do. Feeling brave?'

'What, go to the National Gallery?' laughed Lindy.

'Fool!' I smiled weakly.

Then I told her my idea.

'It's the only thing I can think of now. It means treading on delicate ground. I must say I'm a bit scared – and Sarah wouldn't like it if she found out.'

Lindy looked thoughtful.

'It's worth a try,' she said. 'Of course, we'll probably get the door slammed in our faces. Tell you what – ' She smiled. 'I'll feel a lot braver when I've had some dinner. I don't know about you, but I'm starving.'

'Me too!'

'I'll meet you up there, outside the gates. After we've been home and had our lunch.'

'Will you really?' I took a deep breath and looked at my watch. 'What time? Half-past two?'

'Half-past two it is, then.'

I raced home and had lunch – sausages and chips and baked beans, with ice cream to follow.

'Isn't Sarah back?' I asked Mum.

'No, she's still at Mrs Brewster's.'

Sarah hadn't come back from her walk last night. Instead she'd phoned to say she'd been invited to stay

81

the night with Roy's mum. Mrs Brewster lived on her own and had no doubt got a bit lonely with Roy away on his course all week. And Sarah had probably jumped at the chance to escape us all for a while.

'I expect she'll stay there now till Roy gets back. He's due back this afternoon some time, isn't he?' I said, scraping my bowl carefully to get the last of the ice cream up. It was chocolate ripple and I didn't want to waste any. 'That'll be nice for her.'

'Perhaps she'll cheer up a bit when she sees him,' said Mum, brightening up herself at the thought. 'I've never seen Sarah mope around the way she has this week. I didn't know she was so serious about him.'

'Yes, maybe,' I said evasively. Mum had got the wrong idea!

Secretly I was thinking it would be no bad thing for Roy to know everything. Surely Sarah would confide in him – and he'd think of something sensible to do? Roy was like that. He might even succeed where I'd failed and be able to persuade her to tell Mum and Dad the whole story. M. Perdou or no M. Perdou.

In the meantime, Lindy and I must continue to try and solve the mystery on our own.

At exactly half-past two we met up again as arranged – outside the gates of Haven college. The gates were open and we wheeled our bikes into the deserted campus.

'Well, here goes,' said Lindy.

'Yes,' I said, looking round. 'Do you think that could be his bungalow over there?'

We were going to try and talk to Mr Blake, the caretaker – Blakey, as Sarah called him.

❀

We didn't get the door slammed in our faces. Mr Blake was out, but his wife was at home and she couldn't have been more friendly.

'Do come in, it's spotting with rain. I'm sorry my husband's out – he's gone to Market Lissenham to pick up a new floor polisher. Come through into the lounge.'

She led us through the hall of the bungalow, a neat modern one that had been built at the same time as the college, then into the cosy lounge. She indicated the sofa and asked us to sit down – a plump, rosy-cheeked woman who obviously enjoyed receiving visitors . . . any visitors, even us. She also obviously enjoyed talking, so we were in luck.

'I can't show you the painting, I'm afraid we haven't got it any more. How did you hear about it?'

'My cousin's friend painted it!' said Lindy, shamelessly. 'I saw her working on it. I thought it was good at the time and my friend Jill, here, is very interested in famous French chateaux, aren't you Jill? She's been dying to get a look at it ever since I told her about it.'

I glared at Lindy. She was really going over the top, as usual.

'We heard that you'd got it in your bungalow, Mrs Blake,' I said shyly. 'What a shame you haven't got it any more.'

'So the chateau was famous, was it?' said Mrs Blake, nodding with pleasure. 'It was a pretty painting. I really liked it when my husband brought it in. He's got a good eye, you know, you'd be surprised. We were both amazed to think that one of the students had just thrown it out with the rubbish.' She glanced at Lindy and smiled approvingly. 'Your cousin's friend is obviously very talented. I was planning to get the picture framed, you know, and hang it up there – '

She pointed to a large blank section of wall above the Minster stone fireplace.

By this time Lindy and I were exchanging puzzled glances. We'd been expecting that all this would be very tricky and delicate, but it wasn't at all. Mrs Blake seemed so happy. She obviously had no idea that Sarah's picture was of any importance – nor that it had been used dishonestly.

'Er – did you know that the picture was a copy of a real French painting, Mrs Blake?' asked Lindy, very casually. 'I think my cousin's friend copied it from the original.'

'Did she really?' said Mrs Blake with interest. 'No, I didn't know that. Ah, no wonder it was such a pretty picture, then. I thought the student had got the whole idea out of her head,' she added, slightly disappointed. 'But of course – ' she smiled at Lindy, anxious not to give offence – 'I still think she did it very well.'

There was a silence.

I was trying to think of the best way of broaching the subject. How strange that Mrs Blake seemed so happy about the whole thing! My lips felt a bit dry so I licked them and then spoke:

'Aren't you disappointed not to have the picture any more, Mrs Blake?' I said. 'What – what exactly happened. Did somebody steal it?'

She just chuckled.

'Good heavens, no! Why should anybody do that?'

'Then – ?' asked Lindy.

'You obviously haven't seen your cousin's friend for a while,' laughed Mrs Blake. 'She's got the picture back now, of course!'

'Got it back?' gasped Lindy.

I just stared at the floor with a horrible sick feeling in the pit of my stomach. I could hear Mrs Blake chuckling, her words washing over my head.

'She'd just thrown it out in a fit of temper with herself . . . so temperamental some of our art students here . . . so grateful to my husband for rescuing it . . . decided she wanted to keep it after all. My husband was telling the principal only the other day. He was interested in the picture too, you know, and was asking what had become of it. He'd popped in about something else. Now, would you two girls like a cup of tea?'

Lindy must have seen the sickly white look on my face because she said no, thanks very much, but we wouldn't stay for a cup of tea. We really had to get going now, and obviously her cousin's friend could show us the painting any time, after all.

We cycled back through the town in silence. Lindy could tell I didn't want to talk. When we passed round the back of the big block behind the civic centre where she lived with her father, she simply said: 'Let's go back to your place, Jill.'

At the top of Newlands Park we dismounted and wheeled our bikes along the pavement.

We stood outside my house for a while, rather than go in.

Lindy was staring up at the windows of the big room that I shared with Sarah. Then she said with a weak smile:

'Your sister doesn't suffer from blackouts, does she, Jill?'

I just smiled feebly in return and shook my head.

'Wouldn't it be funny,' Lindy went on, 'after us turning Haven upside down this morning, if the Perdou painting were in your room all the time. Under Sarah's bed, for instance!'

'Would it?' I said, licking my dry lips. 'What are you thinking, Lindy. Are you thinking that Pudding could have been right all along?'

'Oh, Jill. I was only joking.'

'Well, please don't make jokes like that.'

There's many a true word spoken in jest – that was one of Gran's favourite sayings. Although neither of us realized it at the time, or made the connection, Lindy was getting surprisingly warm.

Then we heard the screech of brakes behind us and a car pulled up.

11

🌸🌸🌸

And Two More Investigators

'Hallo, Jill! Hallo, Lindy!'

Sarah jumped out of Roy's car. She looked more cheerful than she'd looked all week.

'Wait here, Roy. I won't be a minute. I'll just dash upstairs and find the keys.'

Lindy and I exchanged puzzled glances. What did Sarah have to look cheerful about? And I wondered what keys she meant, too.

As usual, Sarah's idea of a minute turned out to be a lot longer.

Roy climbed out of the car to stretch his legs, then came and leant against the bonnet and talked to us. Lindy and I propped our bikes up against the fence now, curious to know what was going on.

'Was the course interesting, Roy?' I asked. 'Did you enjoy it?'

'Mmm,' he said. He was obviously preoccupied and kept glancing towards the house, waiting for Sarah to reappear. 'Fine.'

At last she came dashing out, leaving the front door open. I noticed she'd had a wash and put a different shirt on, and was wearing a touch of make-up.

'Jill!' she said, racing up to where the three of us were standing by the car. She lowered her voice. Mrs

Skeet, our nosy neighbour opposite, was peering out of her window as usual. 'Can you remember where I put Monsieur Perdou's keys? I've been looking for them everywhere!'

'Oh, Sar!' I exclaimed. 'I'll get them!'

I ran through the front garden and into the house and went up the stairs two at a time. Sarah was always 'losing' things in our room and I usually knew where they were. The large key ring with its grubby tag and two keys was in its usual place – hanging on our little notice-board behind the door.

M. Perdou had entrusted the keys of his lodgings to Sarah after she'd visited him at the Clutterhouse Clinic, so that she could collect some books he wanted to read. After that she'd acted regularly as the Frenchman's courier, collecting things he needed from Taplow Street, returning things he'd finished with. It had brought it home to me how lonely his life must be in Haven, his only real friend one of his students.

What did she want the keys for now?

As I handed them to her, I asked her that question.

Sarah and Roy exchanged conspiratorial glances, so I knew at once she'd confided in him about the missing painting and that there was some kind of plan afoot. Then she glanced at Lindy.

'Tell you later, Jill,' she said.

'It's all right, Sarah,' I said quietly. 'Lindy knows – I've told her everything. You said I could, remember?'

'Oh, all right then. But we can't stop long. Roy's had a marvellous idea – we're on our way to visit Monsieur Perdou now, but first we're going to pick up that very old book he's got. You know, the one with his great-grandfather's paintings in. It's in his bookcase, I've seen it. It's got a reproduction of *Le Chateau Perdou* in, remember?'

'You mean you're going to tell him it's been pinched after all?' I exclaimed in surprise. 'I thought you said . . .'

'Of course I'm not going to tell him that!' said Sarah, impatiently. 'He mustn't suspect a thing. We've got to be very careful. But . . . oh, Jill, Roy's being so sensible about everything. It's so obvious when you think about it – '

Roy took hold of Sarah's arm, anxious that they should be off.

He glanced across to our house, as though to make sure that no one could overhear, then said rapidly:

'It's like this, Jill. Whoever took Sarah's painting from the Blakes' bungalow *knew* what it was a copy of – and knew where to find the original. It strikes me it must have been one of Monsieur Perdou's other students, up at the college. Which means that after Sarah returned this book to him – and it was the only time he'd ever brought it to college as far as she can remember – one of the other students must have asked him if they could look at it. And he must have talked to that student about the chateau painting in the book and mentioned that the original was here in Haven – hanging in Les-Jen Lodge.'

'Don't you see, Jill?' Sarah butted in, her cheeks rather flushed. 'We know that at least one student saw Mr Blake rescue that copy I threw away. Were there others? Was there someone who knew it was a copy – and knew where the original was hanging – and so decided to get it back from Blakey and make the switch?'

I said nothing. Lindy cleared her throat.

'Well, anything's possible,' she said.

Sarah turned on her, looking quite indignant.

'Of course it's possible! Roy's put his finger on it straight away! And now we're going to browse through the old book with Monsieur Perdou and try and get him talking. Seeing the picture of the chateau in the book will jog his memory – we'll ask him if anybody else at college liked it. We'll have to be very careful, of course, so he doesn't suspect there's anything wrong . . .'

'Come on, Sarah, we *must* get going now,' said Roy, stopping her in full flow. 'We'll miss visiting time if we're not careful.'

''Bye, Jill. 'Bye Lindy!' gabbled Sarah as she climbed into the car. She put her finger to her lips. 'And remember, not a *word* to *anyone* about *anything*.'

Lindy and I stood back on the pavement as the car pulled off. We watched it turn out of the top of Newlands Park, heading in the direction of Taplow Street where the solitary Frenchman had his empty lodgings.

'Two more investigators,' said Lindy drily.

I thought of Sarah's flushed, eager face – cheerful again, blissfully convinced that with Roy's help they were soon going to solve the mystery now. It was – as if I'd ever needed to be convinced! – the face of innocence.

'D'you still think – even jokingly – that the Perdou painting might be under Sarah's bed?' I asked Lindy, with just a very slight edge to my voice.

'Not unless she had a blackout,' Lindy said. That was the second time. 'No, Jill. Of course I don't. But you must admit it's peculiar. Do you think Mrs Blake could have been lying?'

I thought about it, then shook my head.

'Not a chance.'

It was utterly perplexing.

'Coming indoors?' I asked, after a few moments' silence.

'I don't think I will,' said Lindy, apologetically. 'I think I'll go now and do the Saturday shopping for Daddy. And have a good think about the puzzle. *You'd* better go in, though. Look – ' She gave me a shove. 'Your Mum's at the window. I think she wants you for something.'

I wheeled my bike slowly down the path.

'There must be a simple answer!' Lindy called out.

'If you think of it, make sure you ring me,' I replied.

Mum wanted me to do some hoovering. She hadn't seen much of me all day! Dad was pottering about, in and out of the garden, and in a good mood. 'I see your sister's stopped moping!' he said to me. 'She seems quite cheerful again.'

It didn't last long.

About an hour later, the other two investigators returned, Roy and Sarah. I was sitting upstairs by our big bedroom window, elbows on the sill, chin sunk in my hands, when I saw the car draw up outside.

I'd done the hoovering – Tony's room and then ours. Tony was out playing football, even though it was mid-summer, with some friends from Dolphin Avenue.

His room had taken the longest because of the usual clutter all over the carpet – comics, bits of Lego and also, the latest craze, dozens of little pieces of wire to do with electronics. I'd piled everything to one side of the room and then hoovered the patch of carpet that was left.

Our room was tidy. I'd had an odd feeling as I came in; it was slightly eerie. Supposing – just supposing . . . Lindy's joke about Sarah having a blackout – supposing it were true?

Before I switched on the vacuum cleaner I tip-toed over to her bed and peeped underneath. Then, very furtively, I looked in her clothes cupboard as well. I couldn't stop myself.

There had been no sign of the stolen painting, of course. I felt ashamed of myself and rushed round with the vacuum cleaner after that and, when I'd finished, put it outside on the landing.

And now Sarah was back.

Roy just dropped her outside the house and then drove off.

A few minutes later I heard footsteps. She was coming straight upstairs, to our room.

'Hallo, Sar!' I said eagerly, as she came in. 'Did you get anywhere – ?'

'No,' she said. She looked pale and upset. I noticed that she was holding M. Perdou's precious old book in its protective box. She laid it carefully on her dressing table, then doubled back and hung up his key ring in its usual place. 'Oh, Jill, it was awful.'

She sat down on her bed and buried her face in her hands.

Apparently the Frenchman had seemed all right when they'd arrived at the clinic, pleased to see them. He'd been sitting out on the verandah in his dressing gown.

But as soon as Sarah had produced the book of

paintings and shown him *Le Chateau Perdou* and started to chat about it, he'd begun trembling from head to foot and told her to take it away!

'It's some sort of relapse, Jill,' said Sarah, very distressed. 'The nurse came straight away and got him back to bed, and she had to give him a sedative. Roy and I felt guilty about it, but the nurse said not to blame ourselves because he's still very up-and-down: the slightest thing can still upset him.'

'Oh, Sarah, how awful,' I said.

'The nurse says best not to visit him for a while – and to ring through first.' She looked utterly downcast again and, swallowing hard, she said: 'It seemed such a good idea of Roy's, didn't it?'

We sat there in silence for a while. I was trying to screw up my courage to tell Sarah what Lindy and I had been doing. How we'd been to the college today and spoken to Mrs Blake at the bungalow, and the weird thing she'd said – about Sarah wanting her painting back.

I opened my mouth and tried to speak, but the words wouldn't come.

Then the phone rang downstairs and I heard Gran calling:

'Jill! Jill! It's for you. Melinda wants to speak to you.'

12

❀ ❀ ❀

Inadmissible Evidence

'Jill! I'm at home! I've been reading that book of famous trials again,' said Lindy, sounding excited. 'I just had to phone you! Listen, it's inadmissible evidence – !'

'What is?' I asked, startled. I broke off quickly as Tony came charging out from the lounge carrying his football, Mum shouting after him:

'Don't you come home in that state demanding tea. Go upstairs and wash all that mud off!'

''Scuse, Jill,' yelled Tony as he barged past me in the hall, then went thundering up the stairs.

'Start again, Lindy,' I said.

'You can't convict anybody on *hearsay*,' Lindy explained patiently. 'In a court of law it would be inadmissible evidence. Got it?'

'What *are* you talking about?'

'Mrs Blake sounded so knowledgeable, didn't she? About Sarah throwing the painting away in a fit of rage, then wanting it back, and being so grateful to Mr Blake for having rescued it. But it was presumably all *hearsay* – some story that she'd heard from her husband. She mightn't have got all the details right. Some vital piece of information might be missing. For example, Mr Blake might have agreed to put the painting outside the back door for Sarah to

94

collect, while in fact somebody else took it away . . .
Or else –'

'I get you, Lindy!' I said then, suddenly feeling quite excited myself. 'Listen, can't talk at the moment . . .'

That was Sarah coming down the stairs and through the hall now. Mum was calling us all for tea. I waited till she'd passed by into the lounge and closed the door behind her.

'How d'you think we can find out?' I whispered.

'We've *got* to speak to Mr Blake,' said Lindy. 'The easiest thing would be to telephone him. The trouble is Daddy's got a big function this evening and he insists I come and hand round the snacks . . .'

I took a deep breath. This was urgent. Was there something in what Lindy was saying? I *had* to know – as soon as possible.

'It's all right,' I whispered. 'I'll phone him. This evening. I'll do it from the phone box at the top of our road.'

'*Jill*!' That was Mum calling again.

'Are you sure, Jill? We could do it together, in the morning.'

'No. I'll do it. I'll come round in the morning and tell you how it went. Okay?' I had to hurry now. ''Bye, Lindy. Thanks for phoning!'

'Jill, you haven't told me what happened at the nursing home. Are they back?'

'Tell you in the morning – 'Bye!'

I put the phone down just as Sarah reappeared. She took me by the arm.

'Come on, Jill,' she said, wanly. 'Tea-time.' She shot the phone – and then me – a worried look. 'I hope you and Lindy aren't up to anything,' she said, very

95

quietly, almost under her breath. 'Roy will think of some new way of trying to sort things out for me. Don't you *dare* get up to anything. It *won't help*.'

'Of course not, Sar,' I said, innocently.

But I couldn't meet her eye.

No wonder I was all a tremble when I went out to the phone box that night, my hands clammy as I picked up the receiver and dialled the Blakes' number.

Lindy had a good point. Mrs Blake thought she knew the whole story – but did she?

I had to find out. Anything was worth a try.

'Haven 230616.'

That was a man's voice!

Blakey's.

He'd answered the phone.

As the pips sounded, I fumbled to get the coin in the slot and nearly dropped it. Then – click – I was through!

'Hallo?' he said.

My nerve almost failed.

'Mr Blake?' I asked shyly.

'Yes?'

'I – I'm sorry to bother you, Mr Blake, but I was interested in a painting you used to have in your house. I came round with a friend about it this afternoon – '

'Oh, you're one of the young ladies who came to see my wife?' He sounded jovial. I began to relax a little bit. 'Wanted to see that painting one of our students did? Seems to be quite famous. I'm beginning to think I let something good go! Not an old master, was it?'

He chuckled. I was glad that he seemed to be such a jolly person.

96

'I don't know why everybody thinks I'm an expert on that painting,' he continued. 'It was only in the house a couple of hours.'

'Only a couple of hours, Mr Blake?' I said, startled.

'That's right! Didn't the missus explain? The young lady – your cousin, was it? – the one who'd painted it. She came and asked for it back. Really sorry she was, that she'd thrown it away. Did it in a fit of temper. Heard that I had it here – and she wanted it back. For her portfolio. Silly girl! Never mind. All's well that ends well.'

I gripped the phone very tight, that horrible sick feeling in the pit of my stomach again. It was the same story, in every detail. This couldn't be right. *Surely* it couldn't.

'Didn't the missus explain all this to you this afternoon?' Mr Blake asked again, slightly bewildered and obviously wondering what I was phoning about.

'Oh, yes, sort of,' I said quickly. Then clutching at a straw: 'What did she look like, Mr Blake?'

'Who?'

'The – the girl,' I said.

'Oh, you mean your cousin, or was it your cousin's friend?'

'Yes, that's right,' I said quickly.

'Well, I don't rightly know,' replied Mr Blake. He seemed to be racking his brains. 'It was dark. She was waiting outside.'

'But you must have seen her when she came and asked for the painting?'

He seemed to be thinking a bit deeper. It had been a long time ago.

'No. I didn't see her. She was too shy. She felt such a fool. She was waiting outside. She asked her art tutor

97

to knock on the door and get it for her. That's right, I'd forgotten that.'

'Did you actually *see* her waiting outside?' I asked.

'Well, I don't know that I saw her. I just got the painting and gave it to him, so that he could give it to her. M'sieur Perdou, it was.'

My scalp was beginning to feel prickly all over.

'Now look here, miss, what's this all about?' Mr Blake was starting to get a little cross. 'If you want to see the picture why don't you just go and see your cousin about it? She's got it now.'

'I – I'm sorry to have bothered you, sir,' I said quickly. 'I just wanted to make sure. *Thanks*!'

Instantly, he was quite jolly again.

'Put you in the picture, have I? Ho, ho! Cheerio, then.'

And the pips went, cutting us off.

I walked back home very slowly, treading on the pavement cracks one by one, stepping in and out of the evening shadows.

Lindy was right. You couldn't rely on hearsay. Mrs Blake mightn't have got all the details right. Some vital piece of information might have been missing. So true! Clever Lindy.

It occurred to me that Blakey would also have witheld that vital piece of information from Mr Williams, the college principal, when asked what had become of the painting. He wouldn't even have thought it worth mentioning.

No wonder Sarah wasn't being allowed to go back to college yet; no wonder she was still under suspicion.

Blakey had just taken M. Perdou's word for it that

Sarah had been standing out there in the dark, too shamefaced to come and ask for her painting back in person – but asking that her gratitude be expressed to the caretaker for having rescued it from the rubbish pile.

Mr Blake had accepted M. Perdou's word for all that without question.

But that was only hearsay, too. Where was the evidence?

13

❧❧❧

The Painting is Restored

On Sunday morning Lindy and I cycled to the address on that tag on M. Perdou's key ring – number 70 Taplow Street. His road was on the far side of Haven, a part that had been there since the 1920s, long before the new town had sprung up around it. It was due to be demolished some time. The road was a depressing sight, all the more so under the bright summer sky. The terraced houses were run-down and dirty, with paint peeling off the front doors. Some of the windows were boarded up after breakages – there was a vandalism problem in this part of Haven. I knew that some of the houses were no longer inhabited, and those that were tended to have a transient population, families or single people who needed to rent rooms until something better could be found. But M. Perdou had lived there for a long time. It was a grim kind of street for somebody like him, I thought, not much of a place to come back to when the Clutterhouse Clinic finally discharged him. Of course, most of his salary from college went to help out his father in France, who seemed to have made a mess of his life, according to Sarah.

'It must run in the family,' said Lindy tersely, when I confided these thoughts to her. We'd propped our bikes in the passageway down the side of number

70 and were now standing on the pavement surveying its shabby front door.

'How d'you mean?' I asked quickly.

'Well, didn't you say the family chateau had to be sold to pay off their debts – and all the pictures that Jean-Paul had ever painted, as well? The Perdou family seem to have made a habit of going broke and making a mess of their lives. And now – '

'Well, don't let's stand here gabbing, Lindy,' I said, nervously jangling the keys in the pocket of my track suit. 'Let's get on with it. Let's find out for sure, shall we?'

She glanced anxiously up and down the street. But it was still wrapped in slumber, Sunday newspapers, sticking out from letter-boxes, waiting to be taken in; tatty curtains pulled across the rows of windows, shutting out the sun. The inhabitants of Taplow Street didn't appear to be the early-risers-and-off-to-church sort. You could almost hear the snores! Besides –

'It's all right, Lindy! We've got an excuse – remember?'

I held the precious book of old paintings, wrapped in its protective cardboard. I'd snatched it off Sarah's dressing table less than an hour ago, after I'd brought her a cup of tea in bed.

'I'll take this back to Monsieur Perdou's lodgings for you, Sar!' I'd announced breezily. 'I'm going for a bike ride with Lindy and we'll be passing right by there! I'll take the keys – okay?'

'Uh?' Sarah had asked, still half asleep. But I was already halfway out of the room. So she'd called after me: 'Hey, Jill. Be very careful with that book. Don't lose it. He's got a glass-fronted bookcase, you'll see it. It belongs in there. Mind you lock the room up after you! Promise!'

101

'I promise!' I'd called back, already going down the stairs.

Then I'd cycled over to Lindy's, got her out of bed and told her everything. And now here we were, on the doorstep of number 70.

The yale key fitted the front door and it swung open. The other key, the big one, would fit the door of his room. I knew that it was the big room upstairs, the one that faced on to the street. It had been turned into a bed-sitting room, Sarah once told me, with a little cooker and a sink in the corner. He shared the bathroom with the other tenants in the house.

Nobody was about. We walked up the stairs, found M. Perdou's room and unlocked the door. Once inside, we gently closed it behind us and gazed round the room.

The curtains were pulled across and the room was in shadow, apart from a single shaft of sunlight that had found its way through a gap in the curtains, illuminating a huge spider's web that had been spun all around the catch of the locked sash window.

The bed was neatly made. There were two small fireside chairs on one side of the room, drawn up in front of an empty black tiled hearth that had an ugly electric fire standing in the middle of it. No doubt Sarah had tidied up on one of her visits, but it was still a very forlorn looking room with that musty and slightly damp smell that comes when somewhere hasn't been lived in for a long time.

We stood there in silence for a moment. I felt guilty to be there – prying into the seedy loneliness of M. Perdou's life that somehow this room laid bare. Lindy must have felt the same, because she said:

'Poor Monsieur Perdou.'

'I – I'll put this back first,' I said then, holding up the book.

I tip-toed over to the big glass-fronted bookcase in the alcove by the fireplace. It was crammed full of books but I found a gap on the bottom shelf, squeezed the volume carefully inside, then shut the glass doors.

When I straightened up Lindy was still standing just inside the door, looking uneasy.

'Come on,' I whispered. 'It must be here somewhere. We'd better start looking.'

After that, we searched the room at speed – we even looked under his mattress, and in the cupboard under the sink in the curtained alcove where M. Perdou did his cooking.

'It isn't here,' Lindy said at last. 'Hey . . . did you hear something then? It sounded like a car pulling up outside.'

'It *must* be here,' I said. 'He'd never have sold it in a million years – and it's hardly likely to be at the nursing home with him! We've got to find it.'

'Wait, it couldn't be in that bag, could it?' said Lindy suddenly, nodding at a brown leather brief case that stood against the wall by the window. 'No. It wouldn't go in there. It's too big.'

'Is it?' I said. A sudden stirring of memory, a sudden little feeling of recognition rushed through me, though for a moment I didn't know why. 'It'd be miles too big in its frame, but it was taken *out* of the frame, remember, and Sarah's copy put in its place.'

I walked slowly over to the bag and dropped down on to one knee.

Lindy dropped down beside me.

'Come on then, Jill. Open up. We've done plenty of spying already so a bit more isn't going to make much difference.'

But that wasn't why I was hesitating. It was just that the bag had a stiff and difficult clasp and my fingers were trembling. Because now I knew why the bag had given me a feeling of recognition. It was something Sarah had said all those weeks ago, long forgotten – until now.

He was wandering round the civic centre late at night, Jill. He was carrying his big brief case and he seemed to think it was time to go to work! He didn't seem to know where he was and the policeman had to bring him home.

Something else . . . something Lindy had said . . .

Your sister doesn't suffer from blackouts, does she, Jill?

Not Sarah.

But M. Perdou . . .?

'Hurry up, Jill!' Lindy was saying. She sounded on edge. 'Get a move on. I'm sure I can hear someone walking around downstairs.

I swallowed very hard.

'I think the Perdou painting *is* in here, Lindy,' I said. 'Here goes.'

I managed to get the clasp undone. Then I opened the big flap of the brief case and carefully hauled out the contents. Some papers to do with college, and sandwiched between them something bulky, like a canvas . . .

I lifted it out and laid it on the floor, and we both gasped.

'The Perdou painting!' whispered Lindy. 'The chateau!'

I stared and stared at it – the familiar muted blues and greys, the misty long-ago quality: *Le Chateau Perdou*!

'It's beautiful,' said Lindy. 'Beautiful! No wonder he wanted it so much.'

'Sitting here in his room all the time,' I said, in

wonderment. 'Still in his bag. It must have been in his bag that night . . .'

'He hadn't even hung it up,' said Lindy, still staring at the painting.

I heard a creak behind us and looked round.

The door was opening, very slowly.

A figure came into the room, his face like parchment, all grey hair and heavy dark eyebrows and strange, expressionless eyes.

Lindy screamed.

It was M. Perdou, hunched inside his big black overcoat even though it was a summer's day. He stared at the painting, where it lay on the floor between us, uncomprehendingly. There was a man with him, standing just behind in the doorway. Then M. Perdou looked at us.

'What are you doing in my room?' he asked. 'You are Jill, yes? Sarah's sister?'

I tapped the painting with my forefinger.

'We came to find the Perdou painting, sir. You stole it from my friend Polly Pudham's house. We came to get it back.'

He looked at the painting again and very, very slowly his eyes lost that peculiar, blank look. Recognition seemed to dawn.

'I stole it?'

'Yes, sir.'

M. Perdou passed his hand across his brow and his face went a sickly colour. 'I remember . . . yes, now I remember.' He let out a low moan and staggered, as though he were about to pass out.

The other man caught hold of him and helped him over to the bed.

'Lie down a minute, there's a good fellow. Come on, old man. Everything's going to be all right, now. You just see.'

'Hadn't we better get him back to the clinic?' asked Lindy anxiously. 'Hadn't we better get a doctor?'

'I *am* his doctor,' said the man. He glanced down at M. Perdou who was now lying on the bed, head propped on a pillow, eyes closed. He was breathing easily and his face in repose looked suddenly peaceful, released.

'I'm his doctor,' the man continued, 'but I haven't been able to get to the root of his trouble. Perhaps you two girls have found the answer. Yes, I've a feeling you have.'

We stood quietly round the bed. M. Perdou seemed to have dropped off to sleep.

'He had a very bad night,' whispered the doctor. 'He's been very bad since yesterday afternoon.'

'After my sister showed him the book of paintings?' I said.

'Yes,' said the doctor. He glanced at me. 'She was your sister, was she? Yes. That's when it started. It seemed to trigger something off. He was delirious all last night. This morning he begged me to bring him here. He said he had done something wrong, but he didn't know what it was. He was hoping he might remember if I brought him home. I decided to give it a try.'

M. Perdou let out another little moan and then his eyes opened. He turned his head – and fixed his gaze on *me*.

'I remember now. Everything. It is all coming back to me. I would like to tell Jill everything, doctor. Please let me talk about it.'

The doctor gave Lindy and me a nod and put his finger to his lips.

'Talk away,' he said. 'Jill is listening.'

'Jill, when your sister brought her effort to college that day I was unkind to her. It was a nice copy. She had done it well. She had done it to please me. But I felt so angry! It served only to remind me of the original. It made me jealous all over again that Mr Pudham would not allow me to buy it. You are listening?'

I nodded. I was sitting on a chair now, holding the painting on my lap. M. Perdou was speaking hoarsely and rapidly, and we could tell it was helping him to be able to unburden himself at last, to open up a door in his mind that had been locked for far too long.

'She was upset by my criticism – she disposed of the painting with the rubbish, and I saw the caretaker take it away. A student saw him take it to his bungalow. Later, when I was alone, when all the students had gone home, I regretted my harshness. Tenderly, I thought of Sarah's copy and of all the love and effort that had gone into it. I would like to keep it, I thought. As a souvenir. That was my *only intention*. Ashamed that anyone should know about these sentimental feelings, I pretended to the caretaker that Sarah wanted it back, and he gave it to me, unsuspecting. And so I brought it home.'

M. Perdou took a few sips from the tumbler of water that Lindy had put by his bed.

'I placed it on the mantelpiece – over there. For two . . . three days I looked at it. Then – one night – I felt angry all over again. I sat here in my room, seized by a black rage.' He shuddered at the memory. 'Yes! It was all the wrong way round, I told myself. Here am I

107

sitting and gazing at a mere copy of my great-grand-father's painting, his masterpiece. A mere copy! Every blemish in it fills me with anguish. And where is the original? It is here in this very town. It belongs to this fat businessman, this Mr Pudham. He buys my great-grandfather's painting, not because he loves it, but because he thinks it will make money. He does not even look at it. He hangs it in the back lobby! If the copy hung there, full of blemishes, he would not even know the difference!'

Ashamed, M. Perdou dropped his gaze.

'And so, I told myself, the copy, by rights, belongs to *him* – not the original. That belongs to me. It is my heritage! *Le Chateau Perdou* . . . We were a great family once, you know. At least – we were an important family. All my past is contained in that picture! It was painted by someone who was my own flesh and blood. All my life I had searched for one of Jean-Paul Perdou's paintings, as a father searches for his lost child, and now – I told myself – it hangs just one mile away and I can gaze on nothing but a copy!'

'And so,' I whispered, feeling strangely moved, 'you broke into Les-Jen Lodge that night and changed the pictures over?'

He closed his eyes.

'I must have done,' he said, simply. 'I remember nothing. Just the black rage as I sat here – and then, the policeman talking to me in the civic centre and asking if I were lost, and bringing me home. But yes – the proof of what I did is clear to see. The painting was in my bag – now you have it on your lap, Jill. I was in the grips of madness! And all the time I have been at the clinic I have been filled with anxiety and guilt and I knew not the reason!' He paused. 'If I go to prison now it is no more than I deserve.'

'You won't!' said the doctor, firmly. He took the painting from me. 'You weren't responsible for your actions at the time, Monsieur Perdou. If Jill can tell me where to find him, I'll see that this painting is restored to its rightful owner. I'll do it today.'

As Lindy and I cycled home I said:

'M. Perdou was right about one thing. The Pudhams *weren't* able to tell the difference. The copy was hanging in their lobby for weeks, wasn't it? And it was only because that expert happened to come that they found out!'

And Lindy said darkly:

'Restored to its rightful owner? Huh!'

'Shall I tell you something, Jill?' asked Sarah. She had taken the news about the whereabouts of the missing painting remarkably calmly. She was far more interested in news of M. Perdou's condition and the prospect of his making a good recovery now. 'Roy wondered if Monsieur Perdou could have had anything to do with it, but we both agreed it was out of the question. He's a man of *absolute* integrity.'

'That must be what made him so troubled,' I said. 'He'd done something so out of character that night – his mind just blanked it out. But there was a price to pay.'

I looked at Sarah and then said, very slowly: 'Of course, he has no *idea* that the college thought you'd pinched the painting! Or about you being suspended, or anything. Lindy and I didn't think it was the right time to mention it.'

'There's no need for him ever to know!' Sarah said. She thought about it. 'He *mustn't* ever know – or Mum and Dad. And I shall tell Mr Williams that, when I go back to college tomorrow.' She laughed then, eyes flashing with triumph. 'Oh, Jill, isn't it marvellous that I can go back tomorrow! That's not the only thing I shall tell Mr Williams – silly old man. I'm looking forward to hearing him say "sorry" and watching him *grovel*!'

She laughed again and then hugged me, saying:

'D'you know, that almost makes the whole thing worthwhile!'

Sometimes I think my sister's the one who should be in that clinic!

'Will you ever forgive me, Jill?' Pudding asked me on Monday. She was very upset. 'I feel awful now.'

It was nice to think that Pudding and I could be friends again.

Lindy and I watched the final of the Junior Cup that week and cheered when Pudding won it. And yet . . . I knew in my heart that things would never be quite the same again, after what she'd thought about Sarah.

Sarah was back at college, of course. To our relief we learnt that Mr Williams was willing to overlook M. Perdou's lapse, which hadn't really been a lapse at all but, as the medical report explained, a 'symptom of nervous breakdown'. He would remain on full pay until he was well enough to go back to work.

Sarah and Roy visited him at the clinic nearly every day and reported that his health was steadily improving.

In the meantime, Mr Williams contacted Haven social services department who found a new flat for him – a modern purpose-built batchelor flat with its own kitchen and bathroom and its own front door. It faced due south and had a big sunny balcony that overlooked Pettigrew Park. We spent two weekends decorating it for him, Sarah, Roy, Lindy and me. That was great fun. Dad even lent us some of his best paintbrushes and told us we could start on our house next, seeing we had so much energy!

Then one day at school, just before M. Perdou was due to leave the Clutterhouse Clinic with a clean bill of health, something very ironic happened.

Pudding took me on one side during P.E.

'Daddy wants to know if Monsieur Perdou's offer of a hundred pounds for the painting still stands.'

'What?' I said, in surprise. 'You mean he's had a change of heart?'

'Not him,' said Pudding, shamefaced. 'His friend who's an art dealer – the one who tipped him off about Perdou in the first place – now tells him he's backed the wrong horse. Apparently Perdou just traced most of his paintings from Manet's – or was it Monet's? Anyway, Daddy wants to get his money back while he can.'

'*And* a bit more,' I said. 'He only paid fifty for it!' But I was very excited. 'Oh, Pudding, Monsieur Perdou's going to be overjoyed about this. What a marvellous homecoming for him!'

The Frenchman, so Sarah told me, wept with emotion when he heard the news and said he didn't deserve such good fortune – adding that of course it was quite untrue that Jean-Paul Perdou had ever copied Manet's work, and that in fact he'd long been convinced it was the other way round, which was no doubt how the confusion had arisen.

Who knows?

One thing I know for sure is that *Le Chateau Perdou* looked wonderful at the dinner party M. Perdou held for us all in his new flat that summer. Or, as Sarah said in her best French accent, *formidable*!

M. Perdou cut a very distinguished figure that evening, even if his carefully pressed purple corduroy suit had seen better days and the black bow tie didn't quite go with it. His grey hair was combed up at the temples and he looked relaxed and handsome.

He was a superb cook, it turned out. Lindy and I liked the mussels in garlic butter best, but the steak was delicious, too, and the raspberry and blackcurrent water ices (we had both!) mouth-wateringly thirst-quenching. We were rapidly becoming Francophiles as we ate our way through that lot!

Afterwards we sat out on the balcony, drinking French coffee and watching dusk fall over the park. Then Roy switched on the two spotlights he'd fixed up on the sitting room wall, where the Perdou painting hung, so that the misty old chateau seemed to become luminous and the waters of the River Loire to sparkle and move beside it.

M. Perdou glided around the room in its illumination, offering chocolate peppermints round, never once glancing at the picture but every moment getting taller, more erect and more dignified in its presence. It really had been restored to its rightful owner now.

In contrast, I thought that the pictures now hanging in Pudding's house were really rather hideous – childish looking representations of Indian gods with lots of arms and legs busily creating the world. They were the work of one Radha Ray who – according to Mr Pudham's art dealer friend – was *really* on the up and up these days . . .

When I told Lindy about it she just laughed and said she only hoped that Sarah didn't get an Indian art tutor next term.

112